# Contents

Preface / v

1. Chapter One: Who Watched from Afar / 1
2. Chapter Two: Campus Challenges vs Familial Warmth / 21
3. Chapter Three: An Unexpected Encounter / 47
4. Chapter Four: With Clara's Mother / 69
5. Chapter Five: Through Tears / 89
6. Chapter Six: Physical Eyes that Never Met Again / 115
7. Chapter Seven: The Third Eye / 125

# A Quiet Ache

*A Heartfelt Love Story of Sacrifice, Healing, and Hope*

Martin Sunyata

Copyright © 2025 Martin Sunyata
All rights reserved.
No part of this publication may be copied,
reproduced in any format, by any means, electronic or otherwise,
without prior consent from the copyright owner and publisher of this
book.

# Preface

In a world where time can feel like a blur and emotions often go unspoken, there are rare moments where the heart's true voice is heard. This is a story of resilience, love, and the delicate threads that bind us to one another.

Ethan and Clara's lives were shaped by hardship, by the unyielding challenges that life often throws at us. Their journey together isn't one of perfection but one of understanding, deep connection, and quiet strength. Through the turbulence of their own personal trials and the unspoken promises they make to each other, they find solace in the simple act of being present.

This is not merely a story of love, but of two people navigating life's darkest hours, embracing both the joy and sorrow that come with caring for another. Through their shared struggles, they come to realize that sometimes, the greatest gift we can give each other is simply the gift of being there—of being fully present in a world that never stops moving.

As you read their story, may you be reminded that love, in its truest form, doesn't need grand gestures. Sometimes, it's found in the quiet moments—when one soul reaches out to another, asking for nothing in return, except for the chance to simply share a life, however imperfect, together.

*"Nobody has ever measured, not even poets, how much the heart can hold."*

— Zelda Fitzgerald —

# CHAPTER ONE

# Who Watched from Afar

They were classmates in high school—Ethan, 18, and Clara, 17—living in a quiet town in Georgia, nestled among the rolling hills and winding backroads of the southern United States. It was a small town where life moved unhurriedly, where the air was infused with the faint scent of pine and magnolia, and where sunsets painted the sky with hues of gold and rose. The vineyards stretched out like immense green carpets under the sun, their clusters of grapes glistening in the light, creating a picture of serene beauty.

It was on one of those golden afternoons in early spring, the kind of day when the earth seemed to exhale softly with the promise of renewal, that Ethan first truly noticed Clara.

Clara's eyes, bright and wise, carried an air of sadness that seemed to draw others in, compelling them to speak with her as they found themselves gazing into her depths.

***

The schoolyard buzzed with life—students laughing, running, and calling out to one another. Some tossed a football, while others huddled in small groups, trading secrets and dreams. The sun hung low in the sky, casting an amber glow over the scene and stretching shadows across the grass.

From his usual spot on the weathered bench beneath the wide canopy of a willow tree, Ethan sat quietly, his books tucked at his side. He liked this spot; it offered him a view of everything without the need to be a part of it. He was the kind of boy who preferred to observe rather than participate, content to let the world unfold before him.

Today, however, his gaze wasn't wandering. It had settled on Clara.

She stood at the edge of the schoolyard, her chestnut hair catching the sunlight and tumbling in loose waves over her shoulders. She was laughing, her face alight with a joy that seemed almost otherworldly. Her friends surrounded her, but to Ethan, it was as though she existed in her own orbit, as if

# A QUIET ACHE

the world bent its light toward her.

Ethan's heart quickened, though he didn't fully understand why. He had known Clara for years— She had always been there, sitting in the front row while he sat in the back corner of the class, answering questions with quiet confidence. But today was different. Today, she seemed to shine in a way he couldn't ignore.

For a teenager like Ethan, quiet and reserved, noticing Clara felt like stepping into the sunlight after standing too long in the shadows. He didn't know what to do with the feeling, so he did what he always did—he stayed silent, watching from afar.

As the afternoon wore on, Clara's laughter drifted toward him on the breeze, a sound that made him feel both happy and achingly small. He glanced down at his hands, rough from helping his parents with chores around the house, and then back at her, whose world seemed so different from his own.

He wondered what it would be like to talk to her, to hear her laugh up close, to be the reason for her smile. But the thought felt impossible, like reaching hopelessly for a star.

And so, as the school bell rang and the students began to scatter, Ethan stayed in his place, watching as Clara gathered her books and walked away with her friends.

It was in that moment, as the beautiful light faded and the sky began to shift into shades of lavender and gray, that Ethan felt the first stirrings of something he couldn't yet name—a quiet ache, a yearning that would follow him long after that spring afternoon.

Ethan's heart ached with a quiet longing for Clara, a deep, persistent. In every moment of solitude, he felt the emptiness of her absence, as if a part of him had always been waiting for her return.

During break times, he would often see her running barefoot on the grass, her laughter a melody carried by the breeze, while he remained quiet, soft, and never loud. Her hair tumbled behind her, catching the light and glowing like embers. To Ethan, she was like the sun—bright, untouchable, and impossible to ignore. He watched as she bent down to pick a daisy, twirling it in her fingers before tucking it behind her ear. Her movements were unhurried, deliberate, as if the world had granted her the luxury of time.

***

Clara came from a wealthy family, but wealth was no salve for the cracks in her home. Her father was a successful lawyer with a commanding presence, and her mother owned two thriving restaurants, yet their lives were riddled with conflict. Arguments flared constantly between her parents, their voices echoing through the grand, cold halls of their large white house situated on a hill of the town. Her parents were rigid and controlling, which led her to obey them without question, as their demanding jobs required such discipline. She had learned early on to retreat into herself, building walls that even her laughter could not fully conceal. Beneath her radiant exterior lay a quiet sadness that few noticed. She only discovered that participating in activities outside was fun and free from the tension and fear she experienced at home.

In contrast, Ethan's life was modest yet grounded in a comforting warmth of family and genuine friendliness. His family lived in a small, old house on the edge of town. His father worked long hours as a laborer, enduring grueling days in the vineyard, his hands calloused from years of hard toil. His mother, though frail from a rare and painful illness called trigeminal neuralgia, struggled daily with its debilitating effects, but radiated warmth and resilience. Ethan's world was small but steady, a stark contrast to the tumultuous grandeur of Clara's life.

At twelve years old, Ethan had already mastered the art of invisibility, slipping through the cracks of social interactions unnoticed. He found peace in solitude, his world painted in the muted tones of introspection. But later, when Clara came into view, his monochrome existence blossomed into vibrant color.

From his vantage point, he studied her with the curiosity of an artist staring at an unfinished canvas. He noted the way her smile started slow and blossomed like a flower, the way

# A QUIET ACHE

her hands moved—graceful, expressive. He memorized the sound of her laughter, replaying it in his mind like a favorite song. Yet, it wasn't just her beauty that captivated him; it was the lightness she carried, as though she had found a secret the rest of the world had yet to uncover.

Ethan's admiration for Clara wasn't the impulsive infatuation of a teenager. It was deeper, more contemplative, like the quiet reverence one feels in the presence of something sacred. He didn't want to possess her or even be noticed by her. Watching her from afar was enough, like marveling at a distant star. She became his quiet fascination, a muse for his daydreams and the anchor for his drifting thoughts.

He often wondered what it would be like to step into her world, to hear her thoughts and understand the rhythm of her heart. But the thought of approaching her filled him with a paralyzing fear. What would he say? How could he, an unremarkable boy with ink-stained fingers and a penchant for disappearing, hold her attention? The chasm between them felt insurmountable, and so he remained on the periphery, a silent witness to her brilliance.

One afternoon, as he sat in his usual spot beneath the willow tree, he saw Clara sitting cross-legged on the grass, a book balanced on her knees. Her brows knitted in concentration as she turned the pages, her lips moving ever so slightly as if tasting the words. His heart quickened. She wasn't just beautiful; she was curious, thoughtful. The discovery deepened his admiration, but it also deepened his loneliness. How could he share his world with someone who seemed to belong to a realm so far beyond his reach? The stark chasm between wealth and poverty left him feeling withdrawn and saddened.

At home, his room became a shelter for his unspoken feelings. He filled the pages of his sketchbook with her drawings—her eyes, her hands, the way her hair danced in the wind. Each sketch was an attempt to capture the essence of her, though he knew he could never do her justice. He wrote poems, too, though he kept them hidden in a shoebox beneath his bed. Words felt safer on paper than spoken aloud, where they might crumble under the weight of reality.

Clara excelled at everything she touched. Her talent in art was undeniable, her sketches and paintings filling the walls of the school with life. Music came as naturally to her as a gifted talent, and her voice, pure and powerful, often echoed through the halls during performances. Painting was her right hand, and music was her left. She mastered both. He admired her from the sidelines, his heart aching with each passing day, yet he couldn't find the courage to approach her.

As the seasons changed, so did she. She grew taller, her features sharpening into a quiet elegance. But her spirit remained the same—strong, radiant. He watched her navigate the world with a grace that seemed almost otherworldly. And though he remained an observer, his admiration for her deepened with each passing day.

His admiration for Clara was not without its thorns. Watching her from afar, he saw the way others were drawn to her, like moths to a flame. She was kind to everyone, her warmth extending even to the loneliest corners of the schoolyard. His heart ached with a bittersweet longing. He envied the ease with which others approached her, their laughter mingling with hers in the open air. He wondered if she ever felt lonely, if she ever looked beyond the crowd and noticed the boy who watched from the shadows.

***

One day, as the first autumn leaves began to fall, he saw Clara sitting alone on the school steps, her head bowed over a notebook. The scene was so out of character—Clara, the center of every gathering, suddenly solitary. It was likely that she preferred sitting outside rather than staying at home.

He felt a pang of concern, an unfamiliar urge to bridge the gap between them. But his feet stayed rooted to the ground, his courage dissolving under the weight of his insecurities.

Suddenly, he found himself walking toward her as she kept reading the notebook, then he saw her gaze fixed on something distant. His heart pounded so loudly he feared she might hear his approaching. His palms were sweaty, his breaths shallow. He had rehearsed this moment countless times, yet as he approached her, his mind felt like a blank slate. As he was close to her, his heart was like jumping out of his chest. "Hi," he finally managed, his voice barely above a whisper.

Clara turned her head slowly, her expression unreadable. She looked at him as though she were trying to place him, her dark eyes scanning him briefly before flicking back to the horizon.

"Hi," she replied curtly, the single syllable weighed down with disinterest.

He swallowed hard, his fingers clenching at his sides. "I... I noticed you like books," he stammered. "I like... them too."

Clara raised an eyebrow, tilting her head slightly. "Oh?" she said, her tone neither curious nor dismissive, but distant, as if humoring him for a moment.

"Yes," he said quickly, his words tumbling out in a nervous rush. "I... I mean, I like... drawing too. Sometimes I draw things from books... like characters or scenes..." His voice trailed off as he realized he was rambling.

She gave a faint nod, her expression still unreadable. She adjusted the strap of her bag on her shoulder and glanced back toward the cluster of girls waiting for her near the school gate.

"Okay," she said lightly, as though her reply were the end of a polite obligation rather than the beginning of a conversation. She didn't linger to say more, her focus already drifting away.

His chest tightened. He had hoped for a spark, a glimmer of interest, but all he found was a polite wall between them. He forced a weak smile. "Well, um... have a good day," he mumbled, stepping back awkwardly.

She nodded again, her lips curving into a brief, impersonal smile. "You too," she said, and with that, she turned and walked away, her figure blending seamlessly into the vibrant world from which he felt so detached.

Ethan stood there, feeling the weight of her indifference settle over him. Then he walked slowly with his heart heavy with sorrow. Her reaction had cut deeper than he expected, and the weight of it lingered in his chest like a dull ache. Despite his attempts to offer support and understanding, it felt as though all his efforts had been dismissed. Her words, sharp and unexpected, left him feeling helpless and misunderstood. He couldn't help but wonder what had gone wrong, why the distance between them felt so unbridgeable. The sadness wasn't just from her reaction, but from the sense of separation it intensified, as if they were now worlds apart.

He walked home and sat on the old wooden log in front of the house, lost in thought. He hadn't spoken to her in years, not since they were in school together, in the same class. But today, he had dared to reach out to her, only to be met with pain in return. He tried to comfort himself, reminding himself that even the brightest stars have their moments of shadow—that perhaps the chasm between them wasn't as vast as he had imagined.

The small, creaky house felt emptier than usual, its walls seeming to echo the quiet questions that filled his heart. He sat on the log for a long time, staring out at the moonlit fields, replaying their conversation in his mind. And now, even after all these years, she still felt just out of reach.

Whenever he felt sad, he would look at his parents, and it gave him the strength to keep moving forward, and whenever he reached home, he always found his parents tidying up the yard, clearing away the overgrown grass, or cleaning and fixing something in the house... It struck him, as it often did, how they were always occupied with something—never idle, even on their days off, their movements imbued with a quiet sense of peace.

***

It was truly a mystery how Ethan and Filipe, coming from such different origins and family backgrounds, managed to forge a bond so strong. Despite their differences, they stuck together, displaying a maturity that far exceeded their teenage years. Filipe and Ethan had been best friends since childhood. Filipe was short and slightly dark-skinned, with a lively demeanor that reflected his South American roots. In contrast, Ethan was white, tall, and well-built, his frame shaped by years of simple, hard work on the farm, which lent him an air of grounded humility. With roots tracing back to Ireland, he carried a quiet strength and simplicity that reflected his heritage. Their bond was unspoken yet deep, rooted in years of shared experiences, laughter, and struggles. They confided in each other more than they did with anyone else. Ethan would often pour out his heart to Filipe, revealing his dreams, fears, and the depths of his unspoken love for Clara. Filipe, with his easy-going nature and empathetic soul, was always there to listen, offering a shoulder to lean on when life felt overwhelming.

Filipe knew Ethan better than anyone—he could read the subtle signs of sadness that remained in his friend's eyes, even when sometimes Ethan tried to hide it behind a smile. He could see how much Ethan longed for Clara, the way his heart ached every time their paths didn't cross or when he watched her from afar, quietly suffering in silence. Filipe often wondered if his friend even knew how much he was hurting, how his unrequited love weighed him down. It was a pain Filipe couldn't fix. He could see it in the way Ethan's shoulders slumped as he gazed at her, hoping for a glimpse of recognition or connection, but she never saw.

Though Filipe tried to keep things light-hearted, a part of him wished he could be more than just a friend to Ethan in those moments—wishing he could somehow ease the burden of the love Ethan carried quietly. It hurt him to see his best friend trapped in his own mind, unable to find a way forward. Filipe had always been more outgoing and had his fair share of crushes, but seeing Ethan go through such emotional turmoil made him feel helpless. Every time Ethan sighed deeply after another failed attempt to reach out to her, Filipe's heart broke a little more. He knew his friend wasn't just hurting from love—he was holding back the need to express everything he had kept bottled up inside.

But Filipe couldn't force anything. He couldn't be the one to fix Ethan's heart. All he could do was stand by, offering advice, small distractions, and encouragement, hoping that someday, Ethan would find the courage to move on or at least let her know how he felt. It was a tough line to walk, watching his friend struggle with love while not being able to intervene directly. But, as his best friend, Filipe knew his role was to stand by, even when it felt like his heart was breaking, too.

***

One beautiful Saturday morning, the air was crisp and fresh, filled with the gentle hum of nature waking up. The bright, gorgeous rays of the rising sun filtered through the towering pines, as Filipe and Ethan made their way along the winding trail to Pine Mountain, a serene spot near F.D. Roosevelt State Park in Southern Georgia. The forest around them was alive with the soft rustle of leaves and the distant call of songbirds, a peaceful soundtrack to their journey.

Filipe carried a small backpack with water and snacks, while Ethan walked with his hands tucked into his jacket pockets. The dirt path beneath their feet was damp from the morning dew, and the scent of pine mingled with the earthy aroma of the woods. The two friends had always found joy in nature, and this morning was no different.

They talked about everything as they walked—school, family, dreams, and the uncertainty of the future. The trail ahead was lined with tall pines, their needles swaying gently in the cool morning breeze. Filipe spoke with his usual enthusiasm, his hands gesturing as he explained his love for nature.

"I want to study something like biology because I love how everything in nature is connected," Filipe said, his voice brimming with passion. "It's like this invisible thread tying everything together—plants, animals, even us, how every plant, animal, insect, and even the soil plays a role in the bigger picture—it's incredible. There's something magical about the way nature heals itself. Nature's given us so much, you know? I want to learn about and understand nature more deeply, possibly working in conservation or research."

Ethan listened intently, his steps slow and thoughtful. "That sounds like a good path, Filipe. Something with purpose." Filipe chuckled. "Well, someone's got to. Besides, nature's been here long before us, and it'll be here long after.

# A QUIET ACHE

There's wisdom in that, don't you think?"

Ethan nodded. "Yeah. There's a kind of balance in nature... maybe something we can learn from. It's been here long, quietly. Whether we notice it or not, it still exists," he said, his voice calm but filled with depth. Filipe understood exactly what his friend meant—it was as though his friend existed quietly, just like nature, without Clara's notice. Unseen, yet present, offering support in subtle ways, much like the natural world that thrived around them, often overlooked but always there. Filipe couldn't help but draw a parallel between the two—how sometimes, the most important things go unnoticed until we take the time to truly see them.

Then Filipe turned the question back to him. "What about you, Ethan?" Filipe asked, glancing at his friend. "You've been working so hard. What's your dream after all this studying?"

Ethan hesitated, staring at the ground as they walked. "I don't know yet," he admitted, his voice quieter. "But... something to help those in need. That's all I've ever wanted, really. To do something beautiful, even if it's small."

Filipe smiled, clapping a hand on his shoulder. "That's enough. You've got the heart for it, Ethan. Whatever you end up doing, I know you'll do it with everything you've got. You have a compassionate heart."

They walked on, their conversation weaving between lighthearted jokes and deeper reflections. Filipe talked about his family's small garden, how his dad taught him to plant tomatoes when he was a kid, and how his mom loved to watch birds from their porch. Ethan shared stories about his parents' advice and their life struggles, their resilience inspiring him to work harder.

The topic shifted to dreams and fears. Filipe confessed that he was afraid of failing, of not living up to his own expectations. Ethan admitted he often felt the same way, the weight of his goals sometimes feeling too heavy to carry.

As they neared the top of the trail, the trees parted to reveal a breathtaking view of rolling hills stretching into the horizon. They stopped to take it in, the beauty of the moment grounding them in the present.

"You know," Filipe said, breaking the silence, "it's okay not to have all the answers. Life's a lot like this trail. Sometimes you don't know where it's taking you, but you keep walking, and eventually, you find a view like this."

Ethan nodded, his heart a little lighter. "Yeah, I guess you're right. We'll figure it out, step by step."

They stood there for a while, the crisp air and quiet serenity of Pine Mountain filling the spaces where words weren't needed.

Filipe turned his gaze from the rolling hills to him, his eyes narrowing slightly with concern. He could see the familiar look in Ethan's eyes—a mix of longing and quiet sadness that had become all too common. Filipe had known him long enough to recognize when his thoughts were somewhere else, or rather, with someone else.

"You're always thinking of Clara, aren't you?" Filipe asked, his tone gentle but direct.

Ethan flinched, as though caught off guard. He didn't answer right away, his gaze fixed on a distant point in the horizon. Finally, he sighed, his voice barely above a whisper. "I can't help it, Filipe. You are the only one who knows me well. I've tried to move on, to focus on other things, but... don't worry—I can manage my studies well. When I focus on my studies, I give it my all." Filipe nodded, letting Ethan's words settle in the air between them. "It's not easy, I know," he said. "But you don't have to carry it all alone. If you need anything from me—anything at all—I'll do my best to help. You just have to say the word."

Ethan managed a small, grateful smile, though his eyes still held a trace of melancholy. "I appreciate that, Filipe. I really do. It's just... what could you even do? She doesn't even know how I feel, and it's been years. I wouldn't even know where to start."

Filipe gave a thoughtful hum, leaning back against a nearby tree. "Maybe it's not about starting anywhere specific. Maybe it's just about taking one step at a time, like we were saying earlier. Whether that step is figuring out how to tell her or finding peace with it, I'll be here to back you up." Then

# A QUIET ACHE

Filipe fixed his gaze on him and added, "Life's struggles might feel like mountains, but you climb them one step at a time." Ethan looked at Filipe, his chest tightening with emotion. "Thanks, man. That means a lot. I just—I don't want to drag you into my mess."

"Ethan," Filipe said firmly, placing a hand on his friend's shoulder. "You're my best friend. If this is what's weighing you down, then it's not your mess—it's ours. Don't forget that."

The sincerity in Filipe's voice struck a chord in him, and he felt a small flicker of hope. The path ahead was still uncertain, but with Filipe by his side, it didn't feel quite as overwhelming.

The two stood watching the scenery for a moment, the wind rustling through the trees as if echoing Filipe's words, offering quiet reassurance that life, like the forest, would find its way. Now, Ethan allowed himself to believe that maybe, just maybe, things could change.

They stood side by side, the landscape stretched out in all directions—rolling hills, vibrant forests, and a sky painted with the warmth of the sun. The quiet sound of the wind through the trees seemed to invite a sense of reflection, and in that serene moment, they felt a deep connection not just to nature, but to each other.

As they gazed at the horizon, the conversation flowed effortlessly, each word coming from a place of shared understanding. Filipe, with his thoughtful gaze, and Ethan, with his quiet intensity, continued to exchange perspectives on life, nature, and what it meant to truly understand the world around them. They spoke of their fears, their hopes, and the ways in which they wished to contribute to something greater than themselves.

Their bond, built on years of trust and shared experiences, felt like the calm after a storm—steady, grounding, and deeply fulfilling. In that peaceful space, everything felt right, as if they were exactly where they were meant to be, together, in tune with the world and each other.

Filipe and Ethan didn't speak much, but the silence was rich, filled with the weight of everything they had shared and everything that remained unspoken. It wasn't awkward; rather, it was a comfortable quiet, one that needed no words to communicate the depth of their bond.

Filipe finally broke the silence, his voice low but steady. "You know, it's in moments like this that I really see how much we take for granted. The beauty around us, the time we get to spend together, and even the simple act of just being present in the moment. I think sometimes we forget how precious it all is."

Ethan nodded, his gaze still fixed on the distant horizon. "Yeah, it's easy to get caught up in the noise of everything. But moments like this remind me of what really matters." Filipe gestured to the vastness before them. "This is what I want to love and protect. Not just for us, but for everyone who comes after."

There was a quiet understanding between them, as if they had both come to the same conclusion in their own time but were now finally able to express it. Filipe's hand brushed against Ethan's, a gesture so simple yet full of meaning. It wasn't a grand declaration, but it was enough—enough to show that, in this shared moment of stillness, they were aligned in their vision for the future. "I don't think I could do it alone," Filipe said softly, almost to himself. "I know I'm not the only one who feels this way, but... sometimes it feels like the world doesn't hear us. Like it's all just... too much. But with you, it feels like maybe, together, we can actually make a difference."

Ethan turned to him then, his eyes meeting Filipe's with an intensity that spoke volumes. "We will. It may not be easy, but I believe we can. I believe in us, in what we're capable of when we come together. We'll find a way."

As the last rays of sunlight embraced them in warmth, they stood there, side by side, feeling the unspoken promise between them. Whatever came next, whatever challenges lay ahead, they would face them together—with the shared knowledge that they had each other and a cause worth fighting for. And in that certainty, in that bond, they found oneness.

Filipe looked at Ethan. "I've been thinking a lot about

what you said earlier," he began, his voice thoughtful. "About wanting to make a difference, about protecting what we have. It's something I've always felt, too. But I guess... I want to understand the *why* behind it all. What is it that drives us to care so much about the world, about each other?"

Ethan turned to him, his expression serious yet gentle. "For me, it's about purpose. I've always felt like I was meant to do something meaningful, something bigger than myself. Something that connects me to the earth, to life itself. I think that's why the idea of protecting nature and contributing to conservation speaks to me so deeply. It's not just about preserving what's here, but about creating a legacy that gives life meaning."

Filipe nodded slowly. "I get that. It's like we're part of something much bigger, and our purpose is to contribute to that. It's not just about the act itself, but the impact it has on everything else. When you think about ecosystems, about the way everything is interconnected, it makes you realize how fragile it all is. How much responsibility we have to keep it going."

Ethan's gaze softened, his eyes meeting Filipe's with quiet conviction. "Exactly. And deep down, it's about giving. When I think about the future, I don't just want to be a part of something—I want to build and give something. Nature is always about giving. A world where people can live in harmony with nature, where we all understand the value of what's around us and of giving. There's meaning in that, something that's worth working for."

Filipe smiled, feeling the weight of the conversation settle into something more hopeful. "And maybe it's not about having all the answers right now. We've got each other to rely on, and together, I think we can figure it out."

The two stood together, the conversation flowing between them like a river, quiet yet powerful. The world around them, still and expansive, seemed to listen, as if it too understood the depth of their resolve. In that moment, they both felt a sense of peace and clarity—this was their purpose, this was their path. And no matter how uncertain the future might seem, they knew they were not alone in it. Together, they had the strength to make it meaningful.

Ethan suddenly turned to Filipe, his expression warm and sincere. "So, Filipe, who is it that you love most right now? Is there someone in your life, someone who's changed the way you see things?" he asked, his tone gentle but probing.

Filipe paused for a moment, looking down before meeting Ethan's gaze. "You know, finding a true lifetime partner... it's not easy," he said, his voice carrying a weight of experience. "Especially when you've grown up in a situation like mine. My mom raised me alone after my dad left when I was just five. I never really got to see what a stable, loving marriage looked like. And it wasn't just my family—there were so many broken marriages around me, people I knew, people I cared about. It left a scar, deep inside me."

Ethan could see the pain in Filipe's eyes, the reflection of past hurt that shaped his views on relationships. "I can imagine that would make trusting people, especially in relationships, really difficult," he said gently.

Filipe agreed, his expression thoughtful. "Yeah, it's hard to believe in lasting love when you've seen it fall apart so many times. It makes you question whether it's even possible. Filipe looked off into the distance, his tone softening. "That's also why I care so much about living things, that's why I want to pursue biology that will give us a deeper understanding of life, from ecosystems to human health," he said. "I feel like I can discover and learn something from them. You know, the creatures and plants all share this world with us. Some living things are quiet, almost unnoticed, but they're often the best teachers. They show us love, patience, resilience, and the simple beauty of existence. I think there's so much to learn from how they live and survive, even when the world around them isn't easy."

Ethan nodded, intrigued. "I see what you mean. It's like they have a wisdom that we don't always recognize, but when we pay attention, it's there."

Filipe smiled slightly. "Exactly. It's a humbling kind of wisdom. And when we understand that, maybe we can live in a way that honors those lessons—whether it's in how we treat the earth or each other." Filipe looked thoughtful, his voice steady but full of meaning. "You know, you can see some people manage to overcome hardships, even in the toughest situations. It's the same with plants and animals—how they can survive after storms or floods, despite everything. My mom, she's one of those survivors. She's been broken, hurt, rejected but she's always found a way to keep going. Seeing her do that has left a deep imprint on me."

Ethan could hear the admiration in Filipe's words, the respect for his mom's strength. "That's really powerful," he said quietly. "It must have shaped how you see the world—how you keep pushing forward, even when things are hard."

Filipe nodded, a hint of gratitude in his eyes. "It did. I guess that's where I get my strength from. She taught me that no matter how much you're hurt or broken, you can always find a way to stand back up. And I carry that with me every day."

Ethan paused, taking in what Filipe had said. "That's amazing. It sounds like your mom gave you a lot of strength, even if she didn't always show it in the traditional way. It must have been hard for her, though."

Filipe gave a small, wistful smile. "Yeah, it wasn't easy for her. But she never gave up. And I think that's what taught me the most—how to keep going, no matter how difficult life gets. She always found a way to stay strong, to keep fighting for what mattered, even when things seemed hopeless."

Ethan leaned forward, his expression more serious. "I think that's something a lot of people could learn from. We don't always see the strength in others, especially when they're going through tough times, but it's there, hidden beneath the surface."

Filipe nodded, a quiet understanding between them. "Exactly. Sometimes strength isn't loud or obvious. It's in the quiet persistence, the refusal to let life's hardships define you. And that's why I try to live by the same principle. Even when it feels like everything's falling apart, you find a way to keep moving forward. It's like... like the plants and animals that survive despite the storms. There's always a way, if you're willing to keep pushing through."

Ethan smiled, clearly moved by the conversation.

"Wow... You've got a good perspective on things, Filipe. I admire that about you."

Filipe shrugged, a humble smile on his face. "I guess I've learned a lot from the things around me—people, nature, even dead leaves and everything. It all teaches you something if you're willing to listen. You know, when you realize that you're always a learner, always open to growing and changing, that's when you truly start to evolve. But the moment we stop seeing ourselves as learners, when we think we've figured it all out, that's when we stop growing—and, in turn, stop living."

Ethan nodded thoughtfully, absorbing his words. "I get that. It's easy to think we know enough, especially when we get older or gain experience. But it's that mindset of always learning that keeps us moving forward."

Filipe smiled slightly, as if recalling the lessons he'd learned from his own life. "Exactly. Life's constantly teaching us something new, whether we're aware of it or not. If we close ourselves off from that, we miss the chance to keep improving, to understand more about the world and ourselves."

Filipe looked at Ethan, his voice quieter now, as he began to share a painful memory. "You know my mom, right? Well, the reason she tragically lost her legs, all the way up to her hips, is because she tried to save me, not thinking of her own life. I was just a little boy at that time, always running around, loving life and having fun. One day, I ran into the street, not realizing a pickup truck was coming toward me. My mom, without thinking, jumped out to pull me back. The truck hit her hard. She went into a coma for two weeks. The doctors couldn't save her legs, so they had no choice but to amputate them."

Ethan was silent, taking in the gravity of what Filipe had just shared.

Filipe continued, his voice thick with emotion. "And after all that, my father left her. He couldn't handle the situation. So, my mom had to raise me on her own. She took on different jobs, always pushing forward, despite everything she had been through. I don't think I'll ever fully understand the depth of her strength, but she did it. She's the reason I try so

## A QUIET ACHE

hard to live with purpose, to honor her sacrifices."

Ethan looked at Filipe with a mixture of admiration and respect. "I was actually planning to ask you about your mom's legs, but I didn't want to intrude, you know?" He paused, gathering his thoughts before continuing. "But hearing you tell her story... she's incredible, Filipe. Truly amazing."

Filipe gave a small, reflective smile. "Yes, she is. She worked so hard, with only two hands—hands of a broken woman. She did everything—never complained, never gave up. Even with all the challenges, she managed to raise me by herself, quietly and content, always finding happiness in my presence, to provide for us. Her strength... it's something I'll never forget."

Ethan said softly, his voice full of deep understanding. "That's why you put so much into your studies, your work, and helping others. You've seen what it takes to survive and thrive, even in the toughest situations."

Filipe thought for a moment, his eyes thoughtful as he responded. "Friend, I've thought about marriage, of course. But... after everything my mom went through, I guess I'm not sure if I'm ready for that. I don't want to risk repeating the same mistakes I saw in so many relationships around me. My focus right now is on giving back, on helping my mom and others who need it. I want to make a difference, and maybe... Maybe one day, I'll be ready for something more personal, something more miraculous. But for now, I can't let myself think about it too much."

Ethan placed a reassuring hand on Filipe's shoulder, his voice steady but full of warmth. "True love can heal, Filipe. It's not always easy to find, but when you do, it has a way of bringing light into even the darkest corners of your life. It's not a fairy tale, and it won't always be simple, but it's worth holding onto. Hope and faith... they create a foundation, one that can give you a future that's brighter than you might ever expect."

Filipe sighed deeply, his fingers absently tracing patterns on the edge of the table. "You know, Ethan," he began, his voice low and heavy, "sometimes I wonder if I'm even capable of that kind of love—marriage, commitment. I've spent so much time carrying the weight of my past, the pain of it. It's like... I don't even know who I am without it."

Ethan leaned back, his expression thoughtful. "I used to feel the same way," he admitted quietly. "For years, I have carried my own wounds as you know, and they shaped me, Filipe. They made me question everything—my worth, my ability to love, even my capacity to be loved." He paused, letting the words hang between them. "But I realized something along the way. Those wounds don't define me. They don't have to be my future."

Filipe looked up, his eyes narrowing slightly, as though searching for truth in Ethan's words. "And you think love just... fixes that?" he asked, his tone laced with doubt.

Ethan shook his head. "No," he said firmly. "Love doesn't fix you. It doesn't erase the scars or make the pain vanish. But it gives you a reason to heal. A reason to try. Love, real love, doesn't ask you to be perfect. It asks you to show up, scars and all, and to grow together."

Filipe fell silent for a moment, his thoughts swirling. "Maybe," he said finally, his voice barely above a whisper. "But I don't think I'm ready for that. Not yet. I need... time. Space to figure out who I am and what I want. I don't want to bring someone else into my fragments until I've sorted myself out."

Ethan nodded, his gaze steady. "That's fair, Filipe. It takes courage to admit that. And it's okay to need time. But don't let the fear of your wounds keep you from believing in love altogether. Sometimes, the right person doesn't just walk into your life—they walk beside you, even through the fragments."

Filipe managed a small smile, though his eyes were still clouded with uncertainty. "I guess it's not just about finding the right person, huh? It's about becoming the right person, too."

Ethan smiled back, his expression warm. "Exactly. And that's a journey worth taking, even if it takes time."

For a moment, both intimate friends were filled with a profound understanding between them—two men, each carrying their own burdens, yet finding comfort in the shared struggle of becoming whole.

Filipe looked down, his mind wrestling with the weight of the years he'd spent in pain, yet Ethan's words seemed to seep into him, slowly shifting his thoughts. Ethan nodded slowly, his gaze soft but firm. "I understand your deep pain, Filipe. It's hard to move forward like that when the pain you've experienced comes from those you love most—your parents. But don't forget, sometimes love can be a healing force, too."

There was a quiet strength in Ethan's words, something that spoke to the depth of his own journey, a journey marked by both loss and the power of resilience. Filipe remained silent for a moment, the weight of the conversation settling into him. As difficult as it seemed, he couldn't help but feel a flicker of hope stir within, as if Ethan's belief in love was starting to rekindle something deep inside him. It was a small spark, but sometimes that was all it took.

Filipe gave a small, appreciative smile. "Maybe one day. But for now, I have a lot of work to do, a lot of lives I want to touch. The future will take care of itself. I always trust that." He paused, looking at Ethan with a quiet conviction. "I've learned that when you focus on the right things, everything else falls into place. At least, that's what I believe."

## CHAPTER TWO
# Campus Challenges vs Familial Warmth

The years rolled on, each one pulling Ethan and Clara further apart in their separate lives. Ethan stayed in the same house in their small town with his parents. During this time, he pushed himself relentlessly in his studies for the admission test and other exams, eventually earning a scholarship to study medicine—A dream that had quietly burned in his heart since his teenage years. In his own way, he hoped to make the world a little less broken—just as he knew he was.

Clara, on the other hand, disappeared from the town like a gust of wind, heading to the city to pursue her passion for painting and music. Her life seemed like a whirlwind of possibilities, far removed from the simplicity of their shared hometown. Ethan would occasionally hear snippets about her from mutual acquaintances—a gallery opening here, a musical performance there—but her world seemed like a distant star, shining brightly yet untouchable.

Despite the distance, Ethan couldn't quite forget her. Every now and then, he'd find himself staring at an old photo from their high school days, the laughter in her eyes frozen in time, reminding him of moments he couldn't quite shake. He wondered if she ever thought of him, if she ever missed the quiet, poor boy who used to watch her from the shade of the willow tree. But then, almost instinctively, he answered himself—she probably never thought of him. With that thought, he closed his eyes, his body still, as if trying to silence the ache in his chest.

For the first four years of medical school, Ethan found the journey challenging, but not beyond his capacity to handle. He was diligent and disciplined, often drawing on the strength of his quiet determination. Yet, there were moments when the weight of it all felt unbearable. Sometimes, after long nights of studying or demanding exams, he found himself wanting to surrender, questioning if he truly had what

# A QUIET ACHE

it took to pursue this path. The thought of the years ahead—demanding even greater focus, sacrifice, and hard work—often left him feeling exhausted and, at times, purposeless.

In those moments of doubt, Filipe, his steadfast and best friend, was always there. Filipe had a way of grounding Ethan with his calm demeanor and unshakeable optimism. "You're not just learning medicine," Filipe would remind him. "You're learning how to give yourself to others in a way few people can. Don't forget why you started this." His words always resonated deeply, rekindling Ethan's resolve to keep moving forward. Though the road was long and unrelenting, Ethan leaned on Filipe's encouragement, his faith in his purpose, and the dream that had carried him this far. He reminded himself that healing others was more than a goal—it was the meaning he had chosen to build his life upon.

***

The sun hung low over the horizon, casting a warm, golden light across the modest house Ethan called home. The house itself was simple, worn around the edges but sturdy—a reflection of the life his parents had built. Its skylight blue grey paint was beginning to chip, and the porch creaked underfoot, but the scent of freshly baked bread and The sounds of nature gave it a warmth no mansion could ever match.

After school, Ethan just wanted to get home. Every day, he stepped through the back gate and into the yard, where his parents were always hard at work. His father, strong despite his years of hard, manual labor, wielded a pair of clippers with practiced ease, trimming the unruly hedges that bordered the property. His mother knelt in the small vegetable garden, her hands buried in the soil as she pulled weeds from between rows of lettuce and tomatoes.

"Welcome home, son," his father greeted, glancing up with a smile. His shirt was damp with sweat, and dirt clung to his calloused hands, but his eyes sparkled with a quiet pride. "How's school going?" The father continued, his voice steady but laced with curiosity. Ethan hesitated for a moment, not wanting to burden his father with his struggles. He forced a small smile and replied simply, "Hi Dad. School is okay, lectures, theories and theories, you know," with a faint smile, trying to sound casual.

Though the answer was brief, his father's sharp eyes lingered on him for a moment longer, sensing there was more beneath the surface. But he didn't press further, trusting that Ethan would open up when he was ready.

Ethan rolled up his sleeves, knowing instinctively there was work to be done. "Dad, what can I help with?" he asked, ready to dive in without hesitation. His mother looked up, brushing a strand of gray-streaked hair from her face. "Son, the firewood needs stacking, and the chicken coop needs cleaning, if you don't mind," she said, turning to her son and speaking loudly enough for him to hear. "Got it, Mom" Ethan said with a nod.

He started with the firewood, arranging the freshly cut logs into neat piles against the side of the house. As he worked, the rhythmic thunk of wood on wood was interrupted only by the occasional chirp of birds overhead. Ethan found a certain peace in these tasks, the kind that came from knowing he was helping to shoulder the daily burdens his parents carried. Besides, he knew that after long hours of sitting and focusing on books, it felt refreshing to get his body moving with some hands-on work.

When the firewood was stacked, he turned his attention to the chicken coop. The hens clucked softly as he cleaned out the old straw and replaced it with fresh bedding. Ethan chuckled as one particularly bold hen pecked at his shoelace, as if supervising his work.

By the time he finished, the sun was dipping below the horizon, painting the sky in shades of orange and pink. Ethan joined his parents on the porch, where his mother had set out a pitcher of iced tea and a plate of cookies.

They sat together, the air heavy with the scent of freshly cut grass and the faint hum of crickets. Ethan's father leaned back in his chair, his hands clasped behind his head. "You know, son," he began, his voice steady and thoughtful, "there's a kind of beauty in this life we live. It's not glamorous, but it's honest."

Ethan nodded, sipping his tea. "I know, Dad. But

## A QUIET ACHE

sometimes I wonder... is this all there is? Just working hard, getting by?"

His mother reached over and placed a hand on his knee, her touch gentle but firm. "Ethan, life isn't about what you have or don't have. It's about the connections you make, the love you give, and the purpose you find in each day. Money comes and goes, but the memories we build together—those last forever."

His father chimed in, his voice tinged with a quiet wisdom. "It's easy to get caught up in the idea that life is about achieving big things. But the truth is, it's the small moments—the laughter at the dinner table, the feeling of dirt under your nails, the satisfaction of a day's work—that give life its meaning."

Ethan listened intently, their words sinking deep into his heart.

He admired his parents for their resilience, their unwavering belief in the simple joys of life. Despite their modest means, they had built a home filled with love and purpose. His father once said, "Education is important, son, but it's not the only way to live a good life. It's how you treat people and how you carry yourself that matter most."

As evening descended, the conversation turned to stories from the past. His father recounted the early days of their marriage, how they had struggled to save enough to buy the house. His mother laughed as she shared tales of Ethan as a mischievous toddler, chasing chickens around the yard. "You were always so curious back then," she said, her eyes twinkling. "Always asking questions, always wanting to understand the world around you."

Ethan smiled, feeling a warmth in his chest that had nothing to do with the tea. "I guess I got that from you two."

They always had something to share at dinner, and these moments became precious. During these times, Ethan learned a great deal from their conversations. The dinner gatherings not only deepened their understanding of one another but also strengthened the bond that kept them closely connected.

The stars began to appear, one by one, dotting the

darkening sky. The family sat in comfortable silence, watching as the world around them settled into the quiet rhythm of night.

As Ethan helped his mother clear the porch and his father secure the tools in the shed, he felt a profound gratitude for the life they shared. It wasn't perfect, but it was theirs—built with love and an unshakable faith in each other.

*** 

That night, as he lay in bed, Ethan thought about his parents' words. He realized that life's meaning wasn't something you found; it was something you created, piece by piece, in the moments you shared with the people you loved. And in that realization, he found a sense of peace he hadn't known he was searching for.

Even though his parents hadn't received much education—his grandparents had been farmers, passing down a life rooted in hard work and simplicity—they lived with a sense of harmony and peace that seemed to transcend the limitations of their circumstances. Their hands were worn, their backs often ached, and their days were physically exhausting, but their spirits remained strong and bright.

Ethan admired their simple lifestyle. Despite the physical toll of their work, his parents always found ways to nurture joy and balance in their lives. His mother would hum old songs while kneading dough in the kitchen, her voice carrying a soothing rhythm through the house. His father often paused from work to admire a sunset, calling Ethan to join him.

"Look at that sky," his father would say, leaning on his rake and pointing to the brilliant hues of orange and purple. "No matter how hard the day's been, the world always gives you something beautiful to end it with."

Their home might not have been filled with material wealth, but it overflowed with something far greater—contentment. It was a life grounded in simplicity, where peace came not from having everything, but from appreciating what they had.

This environment shaped Ethan profoundly. He learned

# A QUIET ACHE

to find fulfillment in the small, everyday moments, to value relationships over possessions, and to see strength in kindness. Though he longed to pursue an education and make the world a little more beautiful, he knew the lessons he had learned at home were as valuable as anything he could be taught in a classroom.

***

Ethan's medical studies were grueling, a constant whirlwind of lectures, late-night sessions, and exhausting clinical rotations. He often found himself drowning in a sea of textbooks, his mind weighed down by complex terminology, diagnostic procedures, and the pressure of knowing that each decision he made could impact a life. The sleepless nights became routine, and the physical exhaustion he felt from hours of study left him feeling like a shadow of himself. There were times when the sheer volume of knowledge and the persistent pace of the program threatened to break him.

But through it all, Ethan pressed on, driven by a deep sense of purpose. Still, it wasn't easy. He often found himself calling home to share his frustrations, seeking true peace in the familiar voices of his parents.

One evening, after a particularly long stretch of sleepless nights, Ethan found himself back in the quiet comfort of his childhood home, sitting across from his parents at the kitchen table. His father noticed the exhaustion in his eyes, the subtle slump in his shoulders. "What's been weighing on you, son?" he asked, setting down his cup of tea.

Ethan sighed deeply, running a hand through his hair. "It's... everything. Medical school is a lot harder than I imagined. I feel like I'm constantly behind, and the pressure is overwhelming. There are days when I wonder if I'm strong enough to keep going."

His mother, ever so gentle, reached across the table and placed her hand on his. "You've always been strong, Ethan. Strength isn't about never feeling weak; it's about getting back up when you do. When life feels heavy, you just need to carry on—step by step. And know that you're never alone in this."

His father nodded in agreement. "Patience, son. Patience

and love—that's what life teaches you. You're going through hard times, but they're shaping you. Like a tree in a storm, it's the tough winds that make it grow stronger. Don't rush through the pain. Take each day as it comes and remember why you're doing this. Your heart's in the right place."

Ethan took a deep breath, their words settling in his mind. He realized that his parents, despite all their struggles, had always carried a quiet strength that came from patience, from knowing that life's trials were part of something bigger. Their advice reminded him of the resilience he inherited from them—strength that wasn't about avoiding hardship but enduring it with love and purpose.

Working in silence alongside nature, Ethan's father found a kind of wisdom that words often failed to capture. The rhythm of the seasons, the patience required to tend the land, the grapevines, and the simplicity of each task taught him lessons that went beyond practical knowledge. As he worked, he reflected on life's deeper truths, applying these quiet lessons into reality with a calm, steady hand. It was in the solitude of nature that he learned the true value of persistence, patience, and the quiet strength required to face life's challenges. This connection with the earth, unspoken yet profound, shaped his understanding of the world and of life itself.

And his mother, though not in good health, was the steady and firm foundation behind him, the one his father often spoke of. Her gentle nature and ability to listen without judgment made her a true partner in every sense. Together, they formed a harmonious duo, balancing each other perfectly through the ups and downs of life. In every challenge they faced, she was a quiet strength, providing the unwavering support her husband needed. Their bond was a beautiful example of how love, patience, and mutual respect could weather the storms of life.

With his parents' comforting wisdom guiding him, Ethan found the strength to push through, knowing that the journey wasn't just about the destination but about the growth that came with every challenge along the way.

Of course, there were times when Ethan's parents raised

their voices at each other during disagreements. But what was truly remarkable was that, before going to bed, one of them would always apologize to the other. They held a firm belief that life was unpredictable and that no one could know if it might be their last night together. For them, every moment mattered, and love always took precedence over pride.

***

In the bustling corridors and crowded lecture halls of the university campus, Ethan couldn't completely escape the attention of his female classmates. It wasn't that he sought it—quite the opposite, in fact. But his quiet determination, his genuine kindness, and the understated confidence he carried naturally drew people to him. Ethan had an attractive, quiet intelligence and a masculine attitude that some girls in his class seemed to admire. Their glances lingered a little too long, and their smiles were warm and inviting. Some were bold enough to strike up conversations after class or sit next to him during study groups, hoping to forge a connection.

Ethan noticed their interest, of course. He wasn't oblivious. But he never encouraged it. His polite but reserved behavior kept most at arm's length. When one classmate—a bright, elegant girl named Melissa—once asked him out for coffee after an exhausting day in the labs, he hesitated before offering her a gentle smile and declining. "I really appreciate it," he said softly, "but I need to catch up on some reading tonight."

Melissa had nodded, masking her disappointment, but Ethan's response was the same with everyone. It wasn't that he didn't value companionship or friendship. It was that his heart already belonged to someone else, even if she didn't know it.

Clara.

Melissa came from a good family—well-educated and grounded in strong Catholic traditions. Every Sunday, they went to church together, and they were often involved in charitable activities, helping and sharing with those less fortunate. Her kindness and warmth made her beloved by many, and it was no surprise that several men admired her.

No matter how much time passed or how far apart their lives had grown, Clara remained in Ethan's mind, a presence that never faded. He couldn't stop thinking about her—her laughter, her grace, the way she used to hum while sketching in her notebook. He often found himself wondering where she was, what she was doing, and if she ever thought of him. Those thoughts had a way of anchoring him, reminding him of why he'd chosen this path in the first place: to make a difference, to find meaning in the service of others.

He didn't want to be distracted. His purpose was clear—to excel in his studies and become a true healer. Love, as he saw it, was not something he could afford to entertain while in the midst of such a demanding journey. And yet, no matter how hard he tried to focus, the memory of Clara's smile and her eyes would sometimes creep into his thoughts, unbidden but welcome. It was as though she had carved a permanent space in his heart, one that no one else could fill.

So he stayed the course, navigating the complexities of his medical training with unwavering determination. He knew that distractions—no matter how appealing—would only pull him further from his goals. And besides, the truth was simple.

Melissa couldn't stop thinking about Ethan. He was always kind yet distant, his focus unwavering. To her, he was a mystery she wanted to solve, a quiet presence that stayed in her thoughts long after they parted ways in class. She tried to get his attention in subtle ways—bringing him notes when he missed a lecture, offering to share her lab materials, or complimenting his answers during discussions. But no matter how much effort she put in, he remained polite but detached, his mind seemingly always elsewhere.

Frustration and determination eventually led her to a bold step later.

Filipe, Ethan's close and empathetic friend, studied at the same campus as Melissa and Ethan, but in a different department, was well aware of Melissa's feelings for Ethan. On the occasion of a friend gathering for coffee, Melissa approached Filipe, under the pretense of needing study help. After a bit of casual conversation, she managed to get Ethan's phone number.

## A QUIET ACHE

During a casual conversation, Melissa confided in Filipe about her admiration for Ethan and her struggle to express her emotions directly. Touched by her sincerity, Filipe decided to give her Ethan's phone number, hoping it might encourage her to take a step forward and share her feelings honestly. He trusted Melissa's good intentions and believed this could bring clarity for both her and Ethan. Deep down, Filipe also wished for his best friend to find happiness and live a lighter life, free from endlessly chasing a distant star. He had acted the way he did because he didn't want to see his friend collapse one day from lovesickness. However, he was wrong in underestimating the strength of Ethan's heart.

*** 

One night, as Melissa sat alone in her small, dimly lit apartment, the weight of her emotions pressed heavily on her chest. The room felt too quiet, the ticking clock on the wall amplifying the emptiness she couldn't shake. She wrapped a blanket tightly around herself, but the chill she felt wasn't just physical—it was the loneliness gnawing at her heart.

Her stomach churned, a mix of nerves and the lingering nausea that had plagued her for days. She reached for the glass of water on the table, but her hand trembled as she lifted it. This wasn't just about feeling unwell—this was about Ethan, the man who occupied her thoughts more than she cared to admit.

As she stared at her phone lying on the coffee table, an idea began to form in her mind.

Melissa, a decent and well-mannered woman, knew that reaching out to Ethan in such a direct way might seem bold, even impolite—something that went against the values instilled in her upbringing. Yet, her love for Ethan was so profound that she found herself compelled to take a step outside her comfort zone. The longing she felt was overwhelming, and despite her hesitation, she couldn't bear to let her feelings go unspoken. It wasn't just courage that drove her—it was the undeniable pull of a heart that couldn't stop missing him.

Her fingers hovered over the screen before she finally found the courage to search for his number. Taking a deep breath, she pressed "Call." The sound of the dial tone felt deafening in the quiet room. When Ethan's voice finally came through, warm and slightly curious, she felt her chest tighten.

"Hello? This is Ethan."

Melissa hesitated for a moment, her voice shaky as she began. "Hi, Ethan... It's... Melissa. I'm sorry to bother you at this hour, but I... I don't feel well. I've been... dizzy, and my fever won't go down. I didn't know... who else to call."

Ethan was silent for a moment, processing her words. Then, with a calm yet concerned tone, he said, "Melissa? How did you get my number? Are you home alone right now?"

"Yes," she replied softly, her voice laced with both guilt and desperation. "I got it from... Filipe. I know I shouldn't have, but I didn't know... who else to turn to."

Ethan sighed quietly, his natural instinct to help kicking in. "Okay, tell me your address. I'll be there soon."

Melissa gave him the details, and when the call ended, she let out a shaky breath. She clutched the blanket tighter around her shoulders, unsure if she had done the right thing. But as she waited, a sliver of hope flickered in her chest—she had reached out, and now she would see him again.

When he arrived at the building, he found himself standing outside her apartment door, hesitating for a brief moment before knocking. The door opened slowly, revealing Melissa looking pale and disheveled, her hair tied back loosely and her eyes glassy. Whatever lingering doubts he had vanished. She didn't look well, and he was here to help. Melissa looked so tired that Ethan had to help her sit on the couch. "Thank you for coming," she murmured. Ethan nodded, ready to tend to her as best he could, still unaware of the deeper emotions that had driven her to call him.

With the final year of his nine years of medical training under his belt, he instinctively knew what to do. He measured her blood pressure—slightly elevated. Her heartbeat was high but steady, while other vital signs appeared normal. After a few more questions, he learned the root of her discomfort: Insomnia from long, restless nights and the mental toll of the pressure from studying.

Yet, beneath it all, there was something else—an emotional weight she struggled to conceal.

Melissa hesitated for a moment, her fingers nervously twisting the edge of the blanket draped over her lap. The quiet hum of the clock in her small apartment room seemed to amplify her heartbeat. She knew this moment was fleeting, and if she didn't speak now, she might never have the courage again.

Her voice faltered, trembling with vulnerability, as she finally admitted, "I've been trying so hard to keep up, but... I can't stop thinking about you, Ethan. It's exhausting, and I feel like I'm caught in this struggle I can't escape."

Ethan froze, his stethoscope still in his hands. Her words hung in the air, vulnerable and raw, but he stayed composed. Balancing compassion with the professional resolve he'd honed over the years, he responded gently, "Melissa, I think your body is telling you to rest—both physically and emotionally. Pushing yourself too hard will only make it worse." He began to realize that Melissa was well aware of her health issues, as she was a diligent and regular medical student herself. He understood that she was using this opportunity not just for medical support, but to get closer to him.

Melissa looked down, her cheeks burning as her words lingered between them. "I know I shouldn't feel this way," she continued, her voice quieter now, "but it's like no matter what I do, you're always there in the back of my mind. I see you in class, hear your voice when I study—it's like I can't let go."

Ethan ran a hand through his hair, his brow furrowed. "Melissa," he began gently, "I... I didn't realize you felt this way."

"I didn't want to tell you," she admitted, her voice breaking slightly. "I know you're focused on your studies, on your family, on everything you've worked so hard for. But I can't keep pretending like it doesn't affect me."

He sighed, his heart heavy. He cared for her as a friend, but he knew his heart was elsewhere—still tethered to memories of Clara, a distant, important figure he couldn't reach. He wanted to respond with kindness, to reassure her without giving her false hope, but the words felt tangled in his throat.

"You're an incredible person, Melissa," he said finally, his tone soft but steady. "You're dedicated, intelligent, and strong. I admire that about you. But... my heart is complicated right now. I'm still trying to figure things out."

Melissa forced a smile, though her eyes glistened with unshed tears. "I understand, Ethan. I just... I needed to say it, even if it doesn't change anything."

Silence fell between them, not awkward but filled with unspoken emotions. Melissa felt both relieved and exposed, as though a weight had been lifted but left a tender ache in its place.

Ethan glanced at her, his voice quieter now. "Thank you for telling me. I know that wasn't easy."

She nodded, wiping her eyes quickly. "It wasn't, but... I feel better now. At least you know." Her gaze softened, but the sadness in her eyes lingered. His mind raced as he searched for a way to comfort her while keeping his focus. Though his thoughts often wandered, he couldn't ignore the pain she carried. It was a quiet weight, something she tried to hide, but he could see it in her eyes, in the way she moved, in the pauses between her words.

She watched him as he gathered his things, his movements deliberate, and she had the unmistakable feeling that he was trying to leave as quickly as possible. Her heart sank, and a knot formed in her throat. She didn't want the evening to end, not like this. Summoning every ounce of courage, she softly said, her voice barely above a whisper, "Could... you stay... here... a little bit,... please?"

Ethan froze mid-motion, clearly caught off guard. He glanced at her, a mixture of surprise and hesitation in his eyes. "Melissa..." he began, his voice uncertain. "Just... for a little while," She added quickly, her tone pleading yet gentle, "I—I don't want to be... alone right now."

Ethan felt that the conversation had already stretched on for too long. It wasn't quite right, yet something in her voice—so vulnerable and genuine—made it hard to refuse.

## A QUIET ACHE

After a long pause, he finally nodded, though awkwardly. "Alright. Just for a little while."

Melissa's face lit up, a soft smile breaking through her pale features. Relief washed over her, and she quickly gestured toward the small couch. "Thank you."

They sat quietly for a moment, the air between them heavy but not uncomfortable. Her happiness was palpable; she felt a flicker of warmth in her chest as she realized he was still here, sitting across from her.

Breaking the silence, Ethan asked, "Did you eat anything before?" His voice was calm, with a touch of concern. She shook her head, her eyes avoiding his. "Not really. I didn't feel like eating." He frowned, his expression softening with concern. "You need to take care of yourself, Melissa. Skipping meals won't help you recover."

She offered a weak smile, her shoulders slumping as she leaned back slightly. "I know... It's just hard sometimes." Ethan nodded, his gaze filled with understanding. "I get it," he said, his voice gentle. "We're both in a field where we know how important it is to take care of ourselves, yet we often forget to practice what we preach. But your body needs fuel to keep going, especially when you're this worn out."

Melissa sighed, her eyes flicking to the window, as if searching for something beyond the words they were exchanging. "I just feel like there's always something else demanding my attention," she confessed quietly.

Ethan leaned forward slightly, a faint smile touching his lips. "You're not alone in that. But you have to remember, you can't help anyone else if you're not taking care of yourself first." She didn't want to answer, knowing those were thoughts everyone already understood. A quiet moment settled between them, the silence speaking volumes.

To fill the silence, Ethan asked, "So, how are you finding the subject we're studying now?"

Melissa's face brightened slightly, glad for the shift in topic. "It's tough," she admitted, "but also fascinating. I've been struggling with some of the material, though. Especially the pathology chapters—they're so dense, and I feel like I'm always behind."

His brow furrowed as he listened intently. "Yeah, it's not easy. I think everyone feels that way sometimes. But you're doing fine, Melissa. Just take it easy."

She looked at him, her eyes softening. "Thanks, Ethan. That means a lot coming from you."

The minutes passed, and while the conversation remained light, Melissa couldn't help but feel a sense of contentment she hadn't felt in a long time. Even in her sickness, even in her struggle, Ethan's presence made everything feel just a little bit easier.

\*\*\*

After seeing Melissa at her apartment, Ethan couldn't shake the thought of Clara.

Melissa had short blonde hair that framed her face, and her striking blue eyes seemed to radiate an inner brightness, filled with wisdom beyond her years. Her movements exuded a quiet calmness, each step measured and graceful, as if every one was purposeful, rooted in a deep understanding of the surroundings around her. Her presence had a quiet confidence, and it wasn't just in the way she looked, but in the way she carried herself—effortless yet purposeful. Ethan deeply understood her situation because, in a way, it mirrored his own. It was one-sided love, and the weight of it felt familiar. He sympathized with her, knowing that feeling of longing without hope.

Yet, despite all the attention and admiration, he couldn't help but feel that Melissa's heart, like his, was caught in the delicate threads of love that seemed to pull her in one direction while the world around her kept moving in another. And just like him, she was left wondering what could have been.

\*\*\*

Sitting on the rectangular stone in his backyard, he wondered, *Has Clara ever felt lonely like Melissa? What has she been doing all these years?* He didn't know anything for sure—just guesses, endless guesses that circled in his mind.

As Ethan sat lost in thought, his father, who was tinkering with the electric saw to fix the old wooden fence, sensed something was off. He looked up and studied his son, sensing a shift in his mood.

"Son, what's on your mind?" his father asked, wiping his hands on a rag.

He hesitated for a moment before responding. "Dad… What do you do when you feel something for someone, but it's not love? What if it's just one-sided?"

His father paused, setting the saw aside, giving him a thoughtful look. "One-sided love, huh?" he mused. "It's not easy. But, sometimes, you need to be honest with yourself about how you feel. If it's love, you give without expecting. If it's not, you let it go, but always with respect."

Ethan nodded, taking in his father's words. The quiet wisdom his father shared was always grounding, but the feelings for Clara still lingered—unresolved and heavy in his heart.

***

This Saturday marked his father's 65th birthday. The small family of three came together to celebrate, in a humble but heartfelt way. The celebration was simple, yet filled with warmth, laughter, and teasing. They shared stories, recalled memories, and enjoyed each other's company.

As they sat around the table, his father's voice softened, and he started to talk about the time before he and his wife were married. "Your mother was so shy back then," he said, his eyes twinkling with nostalgia. "I was timid too. It was a different time, you know—simple, honest, and naive. We didn't have all this modern technology. People actually spent time together, really got to know each other, without the distractions of screens. We found joy in the little things, in each other's company. At that time, neighbors could walk from house to house with ease, always greeting each other like old friends," his father continued, his voice carrying the warmth of memories. "Children in the same neighborhood would play together—simple games, but filled with so much joy. There was a trust between us all. As a family in need, we were always ready to give help without reservation, knowing that if the roles were ever reversed, the same kindness would be returned. It wasn't about having much, but about sharing what little we had, knowing that we were all in this together."

"But today, it's different," his father said with a sigh, a trace of sadness in his voice. "We hardly know the names of the people living in the house next door. Everyone is so busy, so caught up in their own worlds, that the simple act of greeting a neighbor feels like a forgotten tradition. We've become so absorbed in our screens, in our own lives, that the sense of community and connection has slipped away. The spirit of helping one another without hesitation, the quiet trust that once existed, has become harder to find. It's a strange thing, how much we've lost, even as we've gained so much in the name of progress."

Ethan smiled at the memory, but then his father's tone shifted slightly. "You know, Ethan, your mother and I have been wondering... We haven't seen you with any ladies lately. Have you thought about your lifetime partner? About your future?"

Ethan's smile faded a little as he listened, the question hanging in the air. He wasn't sure how to answer, especially when his mind was so occupied with other thoughts— thoughts of a *lady* he could never seem to forget.

Ethan sat quietly for a moment, the weight of his thoughts pressing against his chest. He realized that it was time to share his secret, the deep part of his heart that he had kept hidden for so long. With a deep breath, he looked at his parents—his father, who had always been a steady source of wisdom, and his mother, whose quiet strength had shaped him.

"Thank you for caring, Mom, Dad. I think it's time to tell you both something," he began slowly, his voice wavering slightly. "There's someone I've never been able to forget. Her name is Clara. We went to high school together."

His parents listened intently, sensing the gravity in his tone. "Clara..." His voice trailed off as he recalled the years that had passed. "I don't even know where she is now, or what she's doing. But she's always been there in my heart. I think about her every day." His father nodded, his expression thoughtful. "You've carried this in silence for a long time, haven't you?" Ethan nodded, feeling the weight of his unspoken emotions. It felt strange, almost freeing, to finally

# A QUIET ACHE

speak the truth aloud. "I didn't want to burden you with my feelings," he continued. "But I've never been able to move on from her. It's like... something in me has always been tied to her."

His mother, ever the empathetic one, placed a hand on his. "Ethan, it's not easy to let go of someone who holds such a special place in your heart. But remember, sometimes life takes us on different paths. We can't always predict where they'll lead us." Ethan nodded, taking in her words. He was grateful for their understanding, but he also knew his feelings for Clara had never been straightforward. "I've tried to focus on my studies. I know I need to, especially now."

His father smiled, a knowing look in his eyes. "You're not the first person to feel that way, son. Love can be complex, but you have to remember to live your own life too. If you're meant to be with Clara, it will happen. But don't lose yourself in waiting. Focus on your goals, and everything else will fall into place."

He continued, "So, does Filipe, your best friend, know about this?" Ethan hesitated for a moment, then nodded. "Yeah, Dad. Filipe knows. He's known for a long time. He's always been there to listen, even when I didn't say much. He figured it out without me having to explain everything."

His father smiled knowingly. "That's the mark of a true friend—someone who understands even when words fall short. Hold onto that friendship, dear son, especially in today's world, where everyone is often caught up in their own lives and struggles." Ethan looked at his parents, grateful for their wisdom. Then, with a sigh, he added, "There's also Melissa. She's a classmate of mine, and... she's in love with me. I care for her. She was truly beautiful and generous, but I don't feel the same way."

His parents exchanged a look, then his mother spoke gently, "Ethan, you don't have to rush into anything. Take the time you need. If you're not ready for a relationship, that's okay. Focus on your path, and everything else will make sense when the time is right." Ethan smiled, feeling a weight lift from his shoulders. He felt truly understood, as if someone had seen the secret part of him he had kept hidden.

"Thank you, Mom" he said softly. "I just needed to hear that." His father clapped him on the back. "You're doing just fine, son. Don't let the pressure of love or life distract you. Stay true to your purpose."

Ethan felt a quiet sense of peace. His parents had given him the clarity he needed. Now, it was time to focus on his studies—and on finding his own way, wherever that path might lead.

As the evening continued, the conversation shifted naturally to a range of topics, flowing freely between them. Ethan's parents, though they had never experienced the academic life their son was immersed in, shared insights that only years of hard work, resilience, and faith could bring. They spoke of their own humble beginnings and the lessons life had taught them—the importance of perseverance, kindness, and the deep value of faith.

"Ethan," his father said, his voice steady and warm, "life isn't always about what you achieve on paper. It's about what you do with what you have. Your heart, your faith, your ability to care for others—that's what defines you."

Ethan listened intently, taking in his father's words. He had always known that his parents valued simplicity over status, and now, as he grew older, he was beginning to truly understand why. Their life hadn't been easy—they had worked hard for everything they had—but they had never let go of the values that had guided them through the toughest times: love for one another, respect for their community, and an unwavering faith in God.

"You see, son," his mother added softly, "in all the years of our marriage, there were times we didn't know how we'd make ends meet. But we trusted in God. We prayed, worked hard, and trusted that He would guide us. And you know, He did. Amazingly." The father nodded and continued after his wife's words: "You know, no one could have predicted what would happen after our marriage. No one expected it to fall apart or for us to face the challenges we did once we began living together. We all believed we would have the perfect family. But who can truly know the future? That's why we place our trust in God's hands, knowing deep down that, with

# A QUIET ACHE

His grace, we will find happiness together."

Ethan felt a deep sense of gratitude for the wisdom and strong faith his parents were imparting. They weren't trying to teach him formulas or equations, nor were they trying to steer him toward any specific career or path. Instead, they were teaching him what truly mattered—the importance of faith, humility, and love, all of which had carried them through life's many challenges.

"Sometimes, we get so caught up in our goals," his father said, "that we forget the simple joys of life. Don't lose sight of the beauty of a quiet day or the value of a kind word. You might find that when you least expect it, life rewards you in ways you never anticipated."

Ethan was moved by their words, understanding that what they were offering him wasn't just advice—it was a way of life. They spoke of patience, of taking each day as it came, and of trusting in God's plan. While Ethan's academic world was filled with deadlines and exams, his parents reminded him that the truest success came from living with integrity, with faith, and with love.

"I know you're working hard, son," his mother said gently. "But always remember to nurture the relationships that matter most. No degree or career can replace the value of family, faith, and love."

Ethan nodded, feeling a sense of peace settle over him. In his pursuit of academic success, he had sometimes lost sight of the things that truly grounded him—his family, his faith, and the simple beauty of life.

His father gave him a reassuring pat on the shoulder. "We've got your back, son. You don't have to figure it all out at once. Just stay true to yourself, be patient, and trust that everything will fall into place."

As the conversation drifted into a comfortable silence, Ethan felt the weight of their words settle deep in his heart. He didn't need to have everything figured out right now. What mattered most was his foundation—the love and faith his parents had shown him. With that, he knew he had everything he needed to keep moving forward.

The night continued with laughter and lighthearted

banter, but Ethan felt a renewed sense of purpose. He would take his parents' advice to heart, striving to balance his ambition with the values they had instilled in him. And perhaps, when the time was right, the path toward Clara—or whatever life had in store—would become clear.

As the evening progressed, Ethan's parents began to open up more deeply about their early struggles, stories that had long been buried under the weight of time but were now shared with quiet strength and honesty.

"When we first got married," his father started, his voice tinged with nostalgia, "we didn't have much at all. We had nothing but each other and a dream. All we had between us was a mere $130—our entire treasure." He chuckled softly, shaking his head. "It wasn't much, but it was everything we needed at the time, for several days. We didn't have fancy things or security, but we had faith."

Ethan listened intently, his heart swelling with admiration for the resilience his parents had shown. Their story was one of sacrifice, faith, and a deep commitment to one another. They had been through so much, yet they were still here, together, standing strong in their love for each other and for their family.

His mother picked up the story, her eyes reflecting a painful memory. "And… then we lost… our little girl, your sister, Ethan." She said softly, her voice barely above a whisper. "She passed away from a rare disease at the age of two, and you were nearly four. We were living in a small town at the time, and we didn't have the resources or the medical support we needed… It was the hardest thing we've ever gone through."

Ethan felt a lump form in his throat as he listened to the pain in his mother's voice. His sister, whom he had never known, had been a part of their family's history, yet her memory had been a quiet presence in their home, spoken of only in gentle tones, never too loud, never too frequent.

His father placed a hand on his mother's shoulder, a silent gesture of comfort. The mother looked at his son, with all her love, "but… through all of that, we learned something. We learned that without purpose in life, and… without trust in God, we wouldn't have made it through. It wasn't only the material things we needed."

Ethan sat in silence, the weight of their words sinking in. His parents had experienced a great loss that most parents could never imagine, and yet they had come through it not with bitterness or despair, but with a deep sense of gratitude for the love they still had, and the belief that God had a plan, even in the face of suffering.

His mother continued, her voice steady now, though tinged with emotion. "We didn't have much. We lived in a small, modest home, and there were days when we didn't know where our next meal would come from. But we always had each other. We always had love. And that was the most important thing."

Ethan's heart ached for the childhood he had never known, the sister he had never met, and the struggles his parents had faced, but he also felt a deep sense of respect and pride for them. Despite the hardships, they had built a life together founded on love, faith, and an unbreakable bond.

"Love isn't just about having a good time together," his father said, his voice filled with conviction. "It's about sticking together when things get tough. It's about being there for each other, even when you don't have the answers. It's about trusting that God will provide what you need, when you need it. He is the One who knows each of us more deeply than we know ourselves."

Ethan looked at his parents, feeling a warmth in his chest. Their wisdom was born not from books, but from experience. From suffering. They hadn't just survived—they had thrived, finding meaning in their struggles and drawing strength from the love they had for one another and for God.

"Don't get distracted by what you don't have, son," his mother said gently. "Look at what you do have—the people who love you, your faith, and the opportunity to do good in this world. That's all you really need to live a full life."

Ethan felt a deep sense of peace settle over him as he listened to his parents' words. He knew their struggles had shaped him, but their strength and love were what truly defined them. As they talked, he realized that, while life had never been easy for his family, it had always been rich in the things that mattered most. And it was those things—love, faith, and the bonds they shared—that would guide him in the years to come.

***

The night ended with laughter and lighthearted stories, but Ethan carried with him the profound lessons his parents had imparted—lessons about love, resilience, and the enduring power of faith in the face of adversity. As he lay in bed that night, his mind wandered to Clara, to Melissa, to Filipe and to the uncertain journey ahead of him.

His thoughts drifted back to his parents with a deep sense of admiration and gratitude. His father, now 65, and his mother, 59, bore the unmistakable marks of a life shaped by trials and sacrifices. Their faces, lined with age and experience, reflected the hardships they had endured. Their calloused hands were a testament to years of labor, and their slower movements hinted at the weight of time and responsibility they had carried.

Yet, despite everything, they remained strong. Not in the physical sense, but in their unwavering faith and the boundless love they poured into their family. Their resilience inspired Ethan, reminding him that strength wasn't about the absence of struggle but about enduring it with grace and finding purpose through it all. Time had aged them beyond their years, but their spirit remained unbroken. Despite all they had endured, they were strong—strong in their faith, their love, and their determination to keep their family whole.

They had poured every ounce of their strength into creating a meaningful life, cherishing the love they shared with Ethan and Mary, his little sister, who had passed away so young. Mary's memory, though a source of pain, had also become a wellspring of resilience and purpose. It was her absence that had given his parents the strength to go on, to find meaning in the small, quiet moments of their days.

Now, Ethan understood something he hadn't before. That was why his mother always placed a chair at the dining table, even though there were only three of them.

# A QUIET ACHE

Every dinner, after they said grace, his mother would glance at that empty chair, her eyes soft with an unspoken emotion. It wasn't just a chair. It was Mary's place—a symbol of her presence, her memory, and the love that still bound their family together. That quiet ritual, so small yet so profound, spoke volumes about his parents' enduring strength and the deep well of love they carried within them. It reminded Ethan of what truly mattered and gave him a sense of peace, knowing he was part of something rooted in love and faith.

As a child, he never gave the fourth chair much thought. To him, it was simply another part of the dining table, an unused seat that faded into the background of daily life. He would swing his legs beneath the table, oblivious to the subtle glances his parents exchanged when setting the table for three instead of four. It wasn't something anyone ever talked about; it was just *there*.

But now, sitting at the table as an adult, with stories he had pieced together over the years, he finally understood its quiet weight. The fourth chair wasn't just a forgotten piece of furniture. His mother had never directly explained it to him, but her actions had always carried the truth. Every evening, she would pause ever so slightly as she passed that chair, her hand sometimes brushing its back as if in greeting. Her gaze would linger there when she thought no one noticed, her eyes distant and tender, as though recalling a moment frozen in time.

To his father, the chair represented strength. He never spoke about the pain, but his hand would tighten ever so slightly on the arm of his own chair when the family sat down for a meal. It was as though he drew courage from that fourth seat, a reminder that they had survived, that they had endured.

And now, as he sat there, staring at the chair with new understanding, he felt a wave of gratitude mixed with sorrow. It was strange how something so ordinary—wood and fabric—could hold so much meaning. The chair had always been more than a chair; it was a bridge between grief and hope, and a quiet reminder that love, even in loss, never truly fades.

Ethan had never truly grasped the depth of the pain his parents had endured. To him, they had always seemed steadfast, their bond unshakable, as though they had effortlessly weathered life's storms. But now, with a deeper understanding, he realized their resilience was born from shared suffering. They had faced profound heartbreak, the kind of pain that could either tear people apart or bind them together irrevocably.

His parents hadn't simply "stuck to each other" out of convenience or habit. They had chosen, time and again, to hold on—to each other, to their love, and to the promise of a better tomorrow. It was in the quiet moments of their struggles, the whispered apologies after heated arguments, and the unwavering support in times of doubt that their bond had been forged.

Ethan now understood that their strength as a couple wasn't just a result of love—it was the product of pain endured together, sacrifices made for one another, and a shared commitment to rise above the trials life had thrown their way. It wasn't perfection that kept them together but their ability to find meaning in their suffering and transform it into a foundation of unshakable unity. Their love was not just a feeling—it was an enduring act of will, a testament to the power of facing pain together and emerging stronger on the other side.

Ethan now saw it for what it was—a symbol of enduring love, of remembering someone who was gone but not forgotten. And in that quiet, sacred gesture, his parents had shown him that love didn't end when someone left. It remained, in the small acts, the quiet moments, and the spaces they left open, waiting.

Then Ethan thought about how faith in God had become the realization his parents clung to through their hardships. It wasn't something they had always spoken about openly, but it was present in the way they lived, in the quiet strength they displayed during their darkest moments. Their faith was not born out of ease or comfort—it was forged in the fire of their trials, a profound understanding that there was something greater holding them together when they felt like falling apart.

Ethan realized this faith was more than just a belief; it was a deep-seated acknowledgment of purpose, a guiding force that gave their struggles meaning. It transcended human love, grounding them in something eternal and unshakable. It wasn't merely a crutch in times of pain but a source of hope and clarity, an anchor that reminded them of their connection to something divine.

This realization, Ethan thought, was not unique to his parents. It was something deep within every person, a yearning for purpose and belonging that often remained unnamed. People carried it unknowingly, searching for answers, seeking something to hold onto when life became overwhelming. His parents had found it in their faith, a faith that taught them to endure, to forgive, and to love despite the pain.

Ethan felt humbled as he sat there, reflecting on how often people mistake faith for weakness when, in truth, it was the quiet strength that allowed his parents to persevere. It was a faith that didn't demand explanations or perfect understanding—it simply asked them to trust, even when the road ahead was shrouded in uncertainty. And now, as he thought of his own life, Ethan wondered if he, too, could find that same sense of peace and purpose—one that had the power to transform even the deepest pain into something beautiful and meaningful.

Then, he felt comforted, remembering his father's words, *trust that everything will fall into place.*

## CHAPTER THREE
# An Unexpected Encounter

Three years had passed since Ethan's father's 65th birthday, and life had continued its quiet rhythm.

Life is full of surprises that people cannot anticipate. The ordinary days, once predictable, have a way of unfolding into moments that change everything. Ethan knew this truth all too well. For years, he had buried his feelings for Clara, convinced that time and distance had sealed the chapters of his past. But fate, as it often does, had other plans.

On a bright afternoon in downtown, the sun hung low in the sky, painting the park in colors of gold and amber. It was the kind of day that seemed to blur the boundaries between reality and memory, where every shadow carried a whisper of the past. There, sitting alone on a weathered bench under the shade of an old oak tree, was Clara!

Her head was bowed slightly, and the silence around her seemed to match the stillness in her posture. The gentle rustle of leaves and the distant laughter of children playing were the only sounds breaking the silence around her.

Ethan was walking briskly along the path that bordered the park, a brown paper bag in his hand containing medicine for his mother. He had just left the pharmacy nearby, his mind preoccupied with her fragile health and the errands that awaited him. As he turned the corner, his steps faltered. He saw her—Clara.

Yes!

The girl he had watched from afar in high school, the one who had always seemed so out of reach, now sat just a few feet away. For a moment, he hesitated, wondering if it was truly her or just a fleeting resemblance. But when she shifted, her face catching the light, there was no mistaking it. It was her.

Her hair cascaded over her shoulder, catching the sunlight in soft waves. For a moment, Ethan stood frozen, unable to move, as if the sight of her had transported him back in time. She was very different from how he remembered her in high

## A QUIET ACHE

school. Though still beautiful, her eyes carried a weight, a hint of deep sadness that hadn't been there before. For a moment, Ethan considered walking past without saying a word. Perhaps it was just a fleeting moment of sulkiness or an inferiority complex, born from the years she had abandoned him. But no. He realized she didn't know anything about it, and something about her posture—the way she sat so still—made him pause.

His heart pounded with a mix of excitement and apprehension as he spoke softly, "Clara?"

This time, he felt different—stronger, more confident. He wasn't the same timid boy who had watched her from afar in high school. Now, he stood before her as a mature, qualified doctor, having faced the rigors of medical school and the challenges of life. His experiences had shaped him, filling him with a sense of purpose and self-assurance.

Clara was stronger. Yes! but with the quiet strength that came with the passage of time. The carefree vibrance of her youth had evolved into a calm, almost serene maturity. Her features had softened with age, and though there were faint traces of weariness in her eyes, there was also a kind of wisdom and resilience that only life's challenges could bring. The lightness that had once filled her had transformed into something deeper, a quiet grace that made her all the more intriguing.

At first glance, Clara didn't recognize Ethan. Her brow furrowed slightly as she looked up at him, leaning back just a little, her body instinctively withdrawing as though wary of a stranger. She startled, a flicker of fear crossing her face, as if the scar from someone who had often made her feel afraid had resurfaced.

Ethan noticed her hesitation and raised his hands slightly in a gentle, non-threatening gesture. "Clara, it's me—Ethan," he said, his voice soft yet tinged with surprise.

She tilted her head, studying his face closely. For a moment, her eyes narrowed, as though she was trying to summon a memory, searching for a face that felt faintly familiar yet oddly out of place in this setting. Then, slowly, recognition flickered across her face.

"Ethan?" she asked, her voice uncertain but softening. Her posture relaxed a little, though a trace of doubt still lingered in her expression. When she looked at him, she didn't just see the boy from high school, but the man he had become—firm, elegant, with the weight of experience in his eyes. There was no defensiveness or guard left in her, no barriers built around her heart. In that moment, sitting before him, she realized that whatever had once been held back, whatever fears or doubts she might have had, no longer mattered. She was no longer the shy girl who had hesitated to connect with him back then. She was a woman who had lived through her own battles, and the weight of them had given her a new perspective on the world.

Her smile, though faint, was genuine, as if she had let go of any lingering insecurities. "It's really good to see you again, Ethan," she said softly, almost as if surprised by her own words. Ethan smiled back, sensing the warmth in her tone. "You too, Clara. It's been a long time."

For a moment, they simply sat there, the noise of the city fading into the background as they allowed themselves to reconnect. It wasn't just a reunion—it was the meeting of two people who had grown, changed, and experienced life in ways that made the past feel like another lifetime. But now, here they were, meeting again, both of them aware that the past had shaped them into who they were today. The bustling downtown around them was alive with activity—street vendors calling out their wares, tourists snapping pictures, and commuters rushing past. Amid the chaos, two old friends unexpectedly encountered each other, a moment of familiarity and warmth amidst the turmoil.

Clara blinked, her mind spinning as she tried to reconcile the boy she once knew with the man now standing before her. Time had sculpted his features—his face was more defined, his posture steady and self-assured—but his eyes held something unchanged, something familiar that tugged at her memory. "I didn't recognize you at first," she admitted, her voice quieter now, almost apologetic. "You look... different."

Ethan chuckled lightly, his laughter like a thread tying the

# A QUIET ACHE

present moment to their shared past. "I guess time does that. But to be fair, it's been, what... twelve years?"

Clara stared at Ethan in surprise. "Twelve years? Really?" she asked, her voice tinged with disbelief, as if the time had slipped away unnoticed. He nodded softly, his eyes thoughtful. She exclaimed, "Well, time flies!" Her expression was a mix of surprise and reflection, as if the years had passed in the blink of an eye. "I didn't expect to run into anyone I knew here... especially not you," she added, her voice softening as she confessed at last.

The initial awkwardness between them began to melt away, the noise of the city fading into an almost imperceptible hum in the background. Both felt a strange mix of nostalgia and curiosity, as though the years apart had created a bridge they were only now beginning to cross.

Ethan's heart swelled with an overwhelming sense of joy, a feeling he hadn't experienced in years. Yet now, here she was, sitting next to him. Clara, the one who had never truly left his thoughts.

The silence between them stretched, but it wasn't uncomfortable. It felt like the weight of years, unspoken words, and missed connections hanging in the air.

"What brings you here?" she asked, glancing at him.

"I was from the pharmacy over there," he said, lifting the bag slightly. "For my mother. She's been unwell."

Clara nodded, her expression softening. "I'm sorry to hear that. I hope she's alright."

"She'll be okay," Ethan replied, then hesitated before adding, "And you? You seemed... deep in thought, alone here." They began the conversation as though they had met each other often before. Clara let out a quiet sigh, her fingers tracing the edge of the bench. "Just... life, I guess. It has a way of piling up on you." She glanced at him, a flicker of vulnerability in her eyes. "Sometimes, it's nice to just sit and breathe."

Ethan nodded, understanding more than he could put into words. For a moment, they simply sat there, two figures from the past, reunited by chance. The years had built walls between them, but in that small park on a quiet evening, it felt as though those walls could begin to crumble, brick by brick.

As the conversation began to flow, tentative and gentle, Ethan felt something stir within him—hope. Perhaps this encounter was more than just a fleeting moment. Perhaps it was a chance to bridge the distance that had once seemed so vast. He glanced at Clara as they sat side by side on the bench, his nerves softening as curiosity took over. "What did you do after our high school? I can't believe time passed so fast. It's been twelve years now?"

Clara smiled faintly, the corner of her lips tugging upward, though there was a shadow behind her eyes. "Twelve years," she said slowly, as if trying to process it herself. "After high school, I went to art school. It was what I always wanted—to focus on my painting."

Ethan's face lit up with a mix of surprise and admiration. "Art school? That makes sense. You were always amazing at it. I remember the murals you painted for the school competitions. Everyone would stop and just stare."

Clara chuckled lightly, though the sound carried a hint of sadness. She sighed softly, her gaze drifting to the horizon. "Those were simpler times," she began, her voice carrying a tinge of wistfulness. "Art school was... exciting at first. I loved it. Every brushstroke, every color felt alive, like I was painting my future onto a blank canvas."

She paused, her fingers tracing an invisible pattern on the bench beside her. "But life doesn't always go the way you plan. The dreams I had, the ones I thought were so vivid, began to blur around the edges. The more we get into life, the more we realize... Not everything is roses and sunshine."

He watched her closely, the weight of her words settling between them. Her vulnerability was palpable, and he could sense the untold stories lingering just beneath the surface. She offered a faint smile, one that didn't quite reach her eyes. "Don't get me wrong, there were moments of beauty, of joy. But there were also challenges I didn't see coming. Times when I wondered if I'd lost the part of me that once felt so alive." Ethan nodded slowly, his heart aching for the girl he remembered and the woman before him now. "Life has a way

# A QUIET ACHE

of testing us," he said gently. "But maybe those tests are what shape the real masterpiece."

Clara glanced at him, a flicker of gratitude in her gaze. "Maybe," she murmured. "Or maybe they just remind us how much we need to keep searching for what truly matters."

Ethan tilted his head, concern flickering in his eyes. "What do you mean?"

She hesitated, as if debating how much to share. "I had to leave school after three years," she admitted, her voice tinged with regret. "My mom got sick, and I needed to be there for her. It was… hard."

Ethan's chest tightened at her words. "Clara, I'm sorry. I didn't know."

She shrugged, her fingers playing with the hem of her sleeve. "It's life. Things happen. I tried to keep painting when I could, but it wasn't the same."

Ethan wanted to reach out, to say something comforting, but he wasn't sure how. Instead, he said, "You were always so strong. I can't imagine how hard that must've been."

He broke the silence. "But now do you still paint?"

Clara's gaze drifted to the horizon. "Not as much as I'd like. Life gets in the way, you know? But every now and then, I pick up a brush. It's like coming home."

"You should now," Ethan said earnestly. "You're too talented not to. The world deserves to see what you can do."

Clara looked at him, surprised by his sincerity. "Thank you, Ethan. That… means a lot." Since her mom got sick, Clara couldn't leave home. Her mother required round-the-clock care, and she had devoted herself to being there for her, unable to step away even for a moment. But today, she felt the need to step outside for some fresh air. She had arranged for her neighbor to look after her mom for a little while, knowing that her mother would be in good hands, even if just for a brief moment.

As the conversation lingered, the years of distance between them began to feel less daunting. In that small park, with the sun dipping lower in the sky, two lives that had once run parallel seemed to be finding their way back to each other. Ethan hesitated for a moment, gathering the courage to ask the question that had lingered in his mind since high school. "And what about your father, Clara? I remember you used to talk about how proud you were of him. He is always so successful, isn't he?"

Clara's expression shifted, the light in her eyes dimming as she looked down at her hands. She didn't respond immediately, and he immediately regretted asking.

"I guess you didn't hear," Clara finally said, her voice soft and strained. "My father... he passed away."

Ethan froze, the weight of her words sinking in. "I'm so sorry. I didn't know. What happened?"

She exhaled a shaky breath, her fingers tightening around the edge of the bench. "It happened when I was in my third year of art school. He was on his way home late one night... He'd gone out with his colleagues to celebrate winning a court case." Her voice faltered, and she swallowed hard before continuing. "They were at a pub, and he must have been tired—or maybe just distracted. His car... it crashed hard against a tree on the way home. He didn't make it."

Ethan's chest tightened as he watched her, the pain in her voice cutting through him. "I didn't expect it..." he said softly, not sure what else to say.

She shook her head, her gaze distant. "After that, everything fell apart. My mom—she collapsed. She couldn't handle it, and the restaurants were too much for her, and... she's never been the same since. She had been struggling with depression ever since. Most days, she just didn't have the energy to get out of bed. And today, it's like she's here, but not really."

Ethan's heart ached for her. "That must have been so hard—for both of you."

"It was," She admitted, her voice trembling slightly. "I tried to keep up with school, but with my mom in that state, I couldn't focus. I had to leave art school to help out. I thought I'd be able to fix things, to hold it all together, but... I guess life doesn't always work out that way."

Ethan leaned forward, his voice quiet but steady. "You've been through so much. More than anyone should have to. But you're still here, still standing. That says a lot about you."

## A QUIET ACHE

She looked at him, her eyes shimmering with unshed tears. "I don't feel strong, Ethan. Most days, I just feel... lost." Ethan had the intuition that there was something deeper beneath the surface, but he didn't dare press her, sensing it was a wound she wasn't ready to reveal.

Ethan's gaze softened. "You don't have to do it all alone, you know. Sometimes it's okay to let someone help carry the weight."

She gave him a faint, almost wistful smile. "Thank you, I hope so. But I feel like I don't want to reach anyone, I am so tired. After everything, trusting anyone feels like standing on thin ice." She admitted, her voice tinged with a sense of withdrawal, as if a part of her had pulled back from the world around her.

As the sun dipped lower in the sky, the conversation between them deepened, unraveling years of heartache and hidden burdens. And for the first time in a long while, Clara felt a glimmer of something she thought she had lost—hope.

Ethan listened intently as Clara shared, the words weighing heavily in the air between them. He couldn't help but wonder how she had managed to carry the burden of everything after leaving art school, her life seemingly unraveling in so many ways. With her youth, talent and family background, it seemed like she had every advantage, yet the toll it took on her was undeniable.

"So how did you manage?" He asked quietly, his curiosity and concern blending in his voice. "I mean, after you left school... all the responsibilities, your mom's condition... how did you afford everything?"

She looked up at him, her eyes reflecting a wisdom he hadn't expected. She hesitated before responding, her gaze drifting to the horizon as if weighing her own thoughts. "My parents left me more than enough money to live comfortably," she said, her voice steady but with a trace of something deeper beneath it. "After everything happened, I realized... money doesn't mean much in the end. It doesn't fix things."

He frowned, puzzled. "But with money, you could have fixed some things, right? Paid for better treatments for your

*An Unexpected Encounter*

mom, or you could keep the restaurants running..."

Clara shook her head slowly, the faintest of smiles playing on her lips. "After my father passed... everything changed. I used to think money could solve everything, but now I see it differently. It couldn't stop my father from dying or keep my mother from collapsing under the weight of everything. It just... it feels so meaningless sometimes. What's the point if it can't protect the people you love? If it can't give us inner peace we need?"

She paused, her eyes misty. "I've realized it's not about how much you have, but what you do with it, and who you're with. Life is fragile, and all the money in the world can't buy back time or fix a broken heart."

Ethan sat in silence for a long moment, absorbing her words. It was a lesson he hadn't quite expected, but it resonated deeply within him. She had been through so much, yet she had found a clarity he had never imagined.

"Exactly! Before I never really thought about it like that," he said softly, his voice tinged with a new sense of understanding. "I always thought if I just had more... maybe life would be much easier."

Clara's eyes softened, and she met his gaze with a quiet intensity. "I used to think that way, too. But I've learned that the real treasures in life aren't the things we can hold in our hands. It's the connections we make, the love we share, the moments of kindness. Those are the things that shape us."

Ethan nodded, a weight lifting off his shoulders as he realized the truth in her words. The path to happiness and fulfillment didn't lie in possessions or success, but in understanding the people and moments that truly mattered. And somehow, in this small, unexpected encounter, she had reminded him of that.

As Clara spoke, he couldn't help but draw parallels to his own parents. Her words mirrored the quiet wisdom he had learned from them over the years. "My parents always said the same thing," He replied gently. "It's not about what you have, but how you live and who you share it with. They never had much, but they gave everything to each other and to me. They found joy in the simplest moments, even when life was

## A QUIET ACHE

hard. I see that in what you're saying. It's... grounding."

She nodded, her expression softening as if she found harmony in the shared understanding. "It's humbling, isn't it? When life strips everything else away, you realize what really matters. People. Love. Kindness. That's all we can hold on to."

Clara's voice grew softer as she continued, the weight of her past revealing itself in her words. "My parents... they were always so caught up in their business. They were successful, yes, but it came at a cost." She paused, gathering her thoughts, before looking up at him. "We never really had family gatherings. Weekends were the worst. My father would go off to play golf with his colleagues, and my mother was always at the restaurants, making sure everything was running smoothly. There were always customers, always new demands."

Ethan listened intently, his heart aching for her. "So you were mostly alone?" he asked gently. She nodded, her expression distant, as if she were staring at a memory only she could see. "Yes. I didn't realize it then, but looking back, it was like we were all living separate lives under the same roof. The house... it was huge, luxurious, by the lake in downtown—everything anyone could want. But it was cold. Like an ignored castle perched on a quiet, desolate hill," she murmured, her voice carrying a tinge of melancholy. "That's how I feel sometimes—standing tall on the outside, but forgotten and empty within."

He glanced at her, his heart aching at the raw honesty in her words. "But even a forgotten castle still stands," he said softly. "It weathers storms, endures time, and holds memories within its walls. You're not empty. You're just waiting for someone to see what's truly inside."

She turned her head slightly, a faint smile playing on her lips, though her eyes glistened with unshed tears. "Maybe," she whispered. "But it's hard to believe that when life keeps chipping away at you. First my dad, then my mom's illness, then... many things... it's like every brick of that castle is crumbling, and I don't have the strength to rebuild it."

Ethan turned to her, his gaze steady yet tender. "Take

some time and space for yourself," he said.

A single tear escaped, tracing a silent path down her cheek, as she whispered. "It's hard," she admitted. "I cannot leave my mother. She doesn't know who she is. Before, she had spent all her energy collecting money and things, believing they could bring happiness to her family."

He nodded, understanding the weight behind her words. "It's not always easy to carve out that space for yourself, especially with everything you've been through. But sometimes, even the smallest moments—a quiet walk, a few minutes of stillness—can make a world of difference. You deserve that, even if it feels impossible at times," he shared.

For a moment, the quiet surrounded them like a protective cocoon. The rustling leaves and faint chirping of crickets filled the silence as she leaned back slightly, her heart softening under the tenderness in his words. The weight on her shoulders didn't feel quite as unbearable.

Ethan felt a pain of sadness for her. The image of that grand house, so empty despite its beauty, was heartbreaking. "That sounds like a lonely way to grow up," he said quietly.

"It was," she admitted, her voice tinged with sorrow. "There were no family dinners, no conversations around the table. I remember sitting in that big, empty house, waiting for someone to come home, but no one ever did. My parents came back at night, tired and distant, like they were just passing through. They were physically there, but emotionally... they weren't."

Ethan's chest tightened, the sadness in her voice stirring something deep within him. "Did you ever try to get their attention?"

Clara sighed, a bitter laugh escaping her lips. "I did. I thought if I became good enough, if I was perfect, they'd notice me. I excelled at school, at everything they thought was important. But it never worked. They didn't notice, or if they did, it was just for a moment. So I learned to keep to myself."

Her eyes met his. He saw the true depth of her pain. "I don't blame them, though. They thought they were doing what was best for me. But you know, what I needed wasn't

## A QUIET ACHE

really money or things. I just needed them. I needed us to be a family, to spend time together. But the house... it was always just a place to sleep. It wasn't a home."

Ethan was silent for a moment, the enormity of her words sinking in. "I'm sorry, Clara. That sounds incredibly difficult." She gave him a small, rueful smile. "It was. But I've learned to live with it. I had to, after everything happened." She looked down at her hands, her expression softening. "I just wish we had known how to be there for each other. How to actually be a family."

Ethan reached out, his voice full of quiet empathy. "I think you're right. It's not about what you have; it's about being together, being present. But it's never too late to change that."

Clara looked up at him, a flicker of hope in her eyes. "Maybe not. But sometimes I wonder... could things have been different, if we'd had more time? If we had just learned to slow down and be with each other?"

Ethan didn't have an answer for her, but he knew one thing: Sometimes, the most important thing in life was learning to be with the people you love, to stop chasing after everything else, and to truly live. And her journey, full of heartache and loss, was teaching him that practical lesson—one he'd never forget.

Her voice trembled as she continued, her words hanging heavy in the air. "At times, I wonder about my existence in this world. What's it for? Is it just about growing up, learning, working, eating, buying things... and then what?" She paused, as if the question itself felt too vast, too overwhelming. "Is that all there is?"

Ethan felt a deep knot form in his chest. He could sense the weight of her doubt, her struggle with finding meaning in the everyday cycle of life. He wanted to say something comforting, but the depth of her pain left him momentarily speechless.

Clara looked away, her eyes distant and sad. "There were times when I felt so exhausted by it all," she continued quietly, her voice barely above a whisper. "I didn't want to keep going. Sometimes I felt I didn't want to live anymore."

## An Unexpected Encounter

Ethan's heart tightened at her admission, his mind racing to find the right words. "Clara..." he began, his voice full of concern. "I'm so sorry you've felt like that. I can't pretend to understand the weight you've been carrying, but I do know this—you've already made it through so much. Even in the darkest times, there's a light worth holding onto, even if it's faint. You're stronger than you realize, and the world is a better place with you in it."

She shook her head slowly, a sad, almost resigned smile forming on her lips. "I think it's something a lot of people feel, but they just don't talk about it. You get caught up in the grind, in the endless spinning of life's flow and eventually you realize why you're even doing it. It's like you're swept away, and before you know it, you've lost sight of who you are, of what truly matters. You start to feel like you're just... existing, but not really living."

Ethan looked at her, his voice steady but filled with quiet determination. "Don't let the darkness win. I know it feels overwhelming, like it's swallowing everything. But even in the darkest nights, there's always a light waiting to shine through—sometimes small, sometimes faint, but it's there."

She closed her eyes for a moment, letting his words settle into the fragile parts of her heart. "It's hard really," she whispered, her voice barely audible. "Sometimes it feels like the darkness has already won."

Ethan shook his head softly. "It hasn't. It never does, not as long as you keep going. One step, one breath, one moment at a time. You're stronger than you think, Clara. And you're not alone anymore."

His words were a lifeline, a flicker of hope she hadn't realized she needed. For the first time in what felt like forever, she allowed herself to believe that maybe, just maybe, the light wasn't completely out of reach.

His gaze softened as he placed a hand on hers gently. "Your life matters You have so much to offer this world. I think... I think sometimes we all lose sight of that."

Clara's eyes filled with a mixture of gratitude and sorrow. "It's hard to believe that when everything around you feels so empty," she said quietly. "I've been trying to figure out what

# A QUIET ACHE

truly matters. Trying to find something worth living for. But it's like... there's so much noise, outside and inside, and I can't hear the answers."

Ethan squeezed her hand softly, offering her the quiet support she had so longed for. "Maybe you don't need to have all the answers right now. Maybe it's enough to just keep moving forward, one step at a time."

She looked at him, her eyes searching his face for the sincerity in his words. She didn't respond immediately, but something in her expression shifted—just a flicker of hope, however faint. "I don't know if I believe in all of that right now," she admitted, "but... maybe I want to. Maybe it's worth trying."

Ethan smiled softly, his heart aching for her. "That's all anyone can do. Just keep trying, no matter how small the steps. You don't have to have it all figured out. And it's okay to have doubts, to feel lost sometimes. You're not alone in that."

Clara nodded slowly, her gaze dropping to the ground as if processing his words. There was a sense of relief in her posture, like a burden had been shared, if only for a moment.

As they sat together in the fading light of the evening, the quiet between them conveyed more than words ever could. Both had lived through pain, both had struggled with the meaning of it all, but in that moment, they had found a small piece of peace—a quiet acknowledgment that perhaps, just perhaps, they didn't need to have all the answers to keep moving forward.

As holding Clara's hand, Ethan felt the chill of it—a stark contrast to the warmth of the summer breeze enveloping them. Her hand was thin, delicate, almost fragile, and as he held it, he could sense the weight of all the hardships she had endured. It wasn't just the coldness that struck him, but the weariness that seemed to radiate from her touch.

Every scar, every sleepless night, every moment of solitude seemed to echo in the softness of her hand. His heart tightened, a mixture of compassion and sorrow flooding through him. He had known that she had suffered, but in that quiet moment, the reality of it hit him more deeply than ever before.

Clara seemed to sense the tenderness in his touch, her shoulders relaxing ever so slightly, though her expression remained distant. "I didn't realize how much I've been holding onto," she whispered, her voice barely audible. "I guess I thought I could manage on my own, but... I don't know anymore."

Ethan didn't have a perfect answer for her. He couldn't fix what had been broken, but in that moment, he wanted to offer her something more than just words. "You don't have to hold it all in," he said softly. "You don't have to carry it by yourself anymore. I'm here for you."

Her eyes met his, and for the first time, he saw a flicker of vulnerability in her gaze, a quiet longing for something more—something real. He squeezed her hand gently, offering her a silent promise that he would be there for her, no matter how long it took for her to heal.

As they sat in silence, surrounded by the fading echoes of the world around them, Ethan realized that sometimes, just holding someone's hand was enough.

Clara's cheeks flushed slightly, and she quickly withdrew her hand, pretending to fix her hair as if the moment had been too much for her. The gesture felt almost instinctive, as if she were trying to regain control of the situation. Her voice was soft, tinged with a hint of embarrassment.

"I'm sorry to bring all this to you," she said, her eyes avoiding his for a moment. "I didn't mean to unload all of that. It's just... sometimes it's hard to keep it all inside. I guess I've never really talked about it with anyone."

Ethan could sense her discomfort, but instead of backing away, he remained steady, giving her space while still offering his presence. He respected her need for distance, but he also wanted her to know that she didn't have to retreat.

She smiled faintly, her tone shifting as she tried to redirect the conversation. "So... tell me about you," she said timidly, as if the change in subject might give them both a way to navigate out of the awkwardness. "Then what have you been up to all these years?

Ethan felt the shift in the air, the tension easing just a

little, but he also understood that her attempt to change the subject wasn't just to divert attention; it was her way of protecting herself. It was easier for her to ask about him than to keep revealing her own pain.

He took a slow breath, leaning back slightly, his mind racing for the right words. He paused for a moment, considering how much to share. He could see the curiosity in her eyes, but also the hesitation.

He blinked, as if pulled from his thoughts, and he took a moment to consider her question. They had never shared like this in any meaningful way, and he hadn't really reflected much on the years that had passed. He sighed, looking out over the park for a moment before meeting her eyes.

A moment of silence wasn't uncomfortable. Instead, it felt like the two were beginning to understand the weight each had carried over the years. He wanted to tell her that she had always been on his mind since high school, but not now. It wasn't the right time.

Ethan's voice was low and slow, each word carrying the weight of years spent in quiet responsibility: "After high school, I stayed close to home to help my parents. They were getting frailer, and I could see how much the hard work had taken a toll on them. I didn't want them to keep struggling alone. I am their only son."

Clara looked at him, her gaze softening with a quiet empathy. She could feel the weight of his words, the sacrifice he had made for his little family. After a moment of silence, she responded, her voice gentle but filled with understanding.

"I get it," she said quietly. "You didn't want them to be alone, to carry everything on their own. It's... hard to watch the people you love get worn down, especially when you feel like you're the only one who can help."

Her words hung in the air between them, and for a brief moment, it felt like the distance that had once existed between them began to close, replaced by an unspoken bond of shared understanding.

"Besides caring for my parents, I had been pursuing something that's always been deep down inside me," he said. "A subject I had felt drawn to for a long time. Something I believed could give me a sense of purpose, a way to make the world more beautiful."

Clara's curiosity was piqued, and she leaned in slightly, her voice soft with interest. "Oh... what did you pursue?" she asked, her eyes searching his for an answer. Ethan hesitated for a brief moment, then smiled faintly, as if finally ready to share a part of himself that had been quietly hidden. "Medicine," he said, his voice growing more sure. "I've always wanted to help people, to be there for them when they need it the most. Health, to me, is the foundation of everything else—if you don't have your health, it's hard to have anything else."

She listened closely, her heart stirred by the quiet determination in his words. She had always known Ethan as the quiet, caring boy who seemed to put others before himself, but hearing him speak so openly about his aspirations made her see him in a new light.

Ethan sighed, looking out over the park for a moment before meeting her eyes. "I just tried to find a way to make a difference," he began, his voice steady but thoughtful. "I wanted to make those in need a little easier, a little better."

His words came slowly, as if piecing together the fragments of his past. "Even though my family couldn't afford it back then—my parents worked hard, but we were never wealthy—I promised myself that I'd keep going, that I'd pursue my purpose no matter what," Ethan said, his voice quiet but resolute. "I knew it wouldn't be easy, but I couldn't let that stop me. I wanted to help people even if it meant struggling along the way."

Clara listened intently, her eyes reflecting a quiet admiration for his determination. Ethan continued, a faint smile tugging at the corner of his lips. "Now, I'm working at a hospital in a small town not far from here," he said, his voice soft but resolute. "It's a humble place, not much to look at, but it's where I can help. There are a lot of patients, and the town doesn't have enough doctors or nurses. It's hard, sometimes."

Clara nodded, her expression thoughtful. She could hear the quiet pride in his words, the conviction that had guided

## A QUIET ACHE

him all these years. Though his life had not been easy, he had stayed true to his purpose. He had found his path, even if it was one paved with hardship.

She had a thought deep inside her, one she had long suspected. The quiet boy from before, who always seemed to carry something unspoken, must have had more depth than anyone realized. Now, seeing him again, she finally understood the answer to what had once been an unspoken question. Sitting next to him now, she felt something stir within her—a sudden pull, an attraction that hadn't been there before. It was as though, in the years that had passed, he had transformed into someone she could no longer overlook.

"That sounds like... meaningful work," she said quietly, her voice filled with a quiet respect. "It may not be easy, but you're doing something that matters."

Clara tilted her head slightly, curiosity lighting up her eyes. "So, what is your major?" she asked. Ethan smiled faintly, a touch of pride and purpose in his voice as he answered, "Geriatrics." Her brows lifted in surprise, and then her expression softened. "Geriatrics?" she repeated, her tone thoughtful. "That's... not something most people would think of right away. Why did you choose that?"

Ethan hesitated for a moment, as if gathering his thoughts, then spoke with quiet conviction. "Because I've seen how much the elderly are often overlooked, how much they need care, understanding, and dignity in their later years. I've watched people close to me grow old and frail, and I realized I wanted to be there for others in the same situation. To help them, not just physically, but emotionally too."

Clara nodded slowly, her gaze fixed on him, admiration shining through. "That's... really great," she said softly. "It takes a special kind of heart to dedicate yourself to something like that." He glanced away, almost shy under her gaze, and shrugged lightly. "It's just something I felt I needed to do." Ethan nodded thoughtfully, his voice calm yet filled with conviction. "To give back, in whatever way I can. I want to do something for the people in our place. I love working in small towns—places that feel simple, nice, and even a little naive. That's where life feels most real to me, where connections matter, and where I feel I can make the most difference."

Clara leaned back slightly, her gaze drifting to the trees swaying in the distance. "You know," she said softly, "it feels like everyone from our generation wants to leave small towns. You are so profound. Young people always seem to head to the big cities, chasing opportunities, bigger dreams, or just... something different."

Ethan nodded, his hands resting on his knees. "Yeah, I've noticed that too. It's like everyone feels they have to leave to really make something of themselves. Big cities are exciting, sure, but they can also be... overwhelming. Not everyone finds what they're looking for there."

She turned to him, a wistful smile playing on her lips. "I thought about it too, you know. Moving to the city, starting fresh, being part of that rush. But..." She paused, her voice growing quieter. "I think I realized that what I was looking for wasn't in skyscrapers or crowded streets. Sometimes, it feels like people leave home searching for something they can't name, only to realize they had it all along."

Ethan tilted his head slightly, considering her words. "I think that's true," he said. "The city might offer a lot, but it also takes away. The pace of life there—it's so fast. You get caught up in it, and before you know it, you forget the little things that make life meaningful."

Clara agreed, her expression thoughtful. "It's strange, isn't it? The way we're all searching for something... and yet we rarely stop to figure out what that 'something' really is."

The two of them sat in reflective silence for a moment, the noise of the park fading into the background. The conversation felt heavy yet grounding, as if they were uncovering truths they'd always known but never voiced.

Their gazes fixed on the people and buildings around them, yet it felt as if neither of them truly saw them. The world seemed to move around them, bustling with life, but in that moment, they were disconnected, lost in their own thoughts.

Clara's eyes drifted across the park, but her mind was

## A QUIET ACHE

miles away. The laughter of young people, the murmur of passing conversations, the rustling of leaves in the breeze—none of it seemed to reach her. She was there, physically present, but mentally, she was in a place far deeper, far more hidden.

Ethan, too, appeared lost in thought. His eyes traced the movements of people walking by, but it was as if the image before him blurred into nothingness. He didn't see the faces, didn't notice the interactions. He was still caught in the gravity of their conversation, the weight of everything they had shared.

They were both here, yet not really here. Their minds wandered to places they couldn't fully express, lost in a quiet reverie of their own making. It wasn't just the park or the people around them—it was as if the world itself had faded into the background, leaving only the silence and the space between them.

Clara suddenly straightened, her expression shifting as though she'd just remembered something important. "Oh," she said, startled, glancing at the time. "I have to go home to my mom. I am sorry, Ethan."

Ethan looked at her, a little startled, and said, "Of course," his voice soft. "She must be lucky to have you." It was also time for Ethan to return home to care for his mother.

He hesitated, his gaze lingering on her for a moment longer than necessary, as if reluctant to end their time together. "It was... really nice seeing you again," he said, his voice warm but tinged with something unspoken.

Clara nodded, her hands fidgeting slightly in her lap. "Yeah, it was. It's been a long time. I... I hope we can catch up again soon."

Ethan paused, his brow furrowing for a second before he reached into his pocket and pulled out his phone. "Do you want to exchange numbers?" he asked, his tone almost shy.

Clara brightened slightly, her smile more genuine now. "I'd like that." She pulled out her phone, and they exchanged contact information, their hands brushing briefly as they handed the devices back to one another.

As they stood to part ways by their own cars, an unspoken tension hung in the air, the kind that came when neither person wanted a moment to end. The quiet stretched between them, not awkward, but heavy with meaning—years of silence and separation compressed into this fragile reunion. Both hesitated, their feet planted as though rooted by the weight of emotions too vast to express.

Clara fiddled with the strap of her bag, her gaze flickering between Ethan and the horizon behind him. She didn't want to leave, but words failed her. "Take care, Ethan," she said finally, her voice steady but laced with a tenderness she couldn't hide.

Ethan met her eyes, his expression softening. "You too," he replied, his lips curving into a small, almost reluctant smile. His hand twitched at his side, as if resisting the urge to reach out one more time.

Neither turned immediately, but when they finally did, their movements were slow, deliberate, as though their bodies protested the distance now growing between them.

As Clara walked toward her car, her fingers brushed the phone in her pocket. For a fleeting moment, she considered calling him, hearing his voice again before they were too far apart. But she hesitated, savoring instead the warmth still lingering from their conversation. She paused for a moment, leaning against the door as a quiet smile crept across her face. There was a warmth in her chest, a feeling she hadn't recognized in years—something that went beyond fleeting happiness. It wasn't just about Ethan's words or the way he looked at her; it was the way he made her feel seen, truly seen, as if the parts of her she had hidden for so long didn't need to stay in the shadows anymore.

She closed her eyes and took a deep breath, letting the moment settle within her. It was strange, this peace, this soft, unspoken joy that felt so foreign yet so familiar. It was as though something inside her had been dormant, waiting for the right moment to awaken. And now, after years of carrying the weight of brokenness and sorrow, she felt a glimmer of hope—a quiet power that whispered that maybe, just maybe, things could be different.

## A QUIET ACHE

Ethan had reminded her of something she hadn't dared to believe in for so long: the possibility of healing, of connection, of finding strength not just within herself but through another. It wasn't about him fixing her or erasing her pain—it was about the way his presence gave her the courage to imagine a life beyond her struggles.

As she opened her eyes and looked at the horizon, she felt a strange lightness, as if the heavy fog she'd been walking through had begun to lift. It wasn't gone, not entirely, but it was thinner now, letting a sliver of light break through. And in that light, Clara found something she thought she had lost forever—hope.

With her hand on the car door, she whispered to herself, "Maybe it's time to believe again." And as she got into the car, her heart carried the quiet joy of someone who had taken the first step toward something new, something brighter. Something worth holding onto.

Ethan glanced back once, his footsteps slowing as he crossed the park. Their eyes met briefly, and the world seemed to pause. In that fleeting moment, a connection hummed between them, a quiet promise that neither dared to put into words.

When he disappeared around the corner, Clara stood by her car for a moment longer, the cool evening breeze tugging at her coat. The ache of their years apart felt distant now, replaced by a tentative hope that this was not an ending, but the start of something new—an unfinished chapter waiting to be written.

## CHAPTER FOUR

# With Clara's Mother

The afternoon sun filtered softly through the window, casting gentle light across the room where Clara's mother sat in her favorite chair by the fireplace quietly. At 60, she looked much older than her years. Her once-vibrant eyes had dulled, the spark of life buried beneath the weight of time and loss. Her hands, once graceful and strong, now trembled as she clasped them tightly in her lap, as if seeking comfort from the fragile pieces of herself that still remained.

Clara stood by the door, watching her mother with a mixture of affection and sorrow. The years had not been kind to Mrs. Deveroux. She had borne the struggles of life quietly, but the loss of her husband—the love of her life—had shattered something deep within her. She had poured everything into the family's restaurants, sacrificing her health and youth, only for it all to slip through her fingers in the end. The restaurants, once the beloved gathering places for the community, had eventually succumbed to the pressures of the changing world, and with them, her sense of purpose.

Now, Clara was her mother's sole caretaker. She helped her mother with everything—from the most basic tasks, like getting out of bed, to the more difficult ones, like navigating the maze of her mother's memories. Clara's household tasks, nameless and endless, became unbearably heavy for her, but she had no choice. She loved her mother, and with her father's absence, her mother was all she had now.

***

One Sunday morning, Clara invited Ethan over—a simple but thoughtful gesture to give her mother a change of pace. The invitation was meant to bring a bit of light into their quiet home, offering a break from the usual routine and perhaps lifting the otherwise dim atmosphere that had settled over the place.

Now, he knew where she lived. He could hardly believe his eyes—a gorgeous house on the hill, with a breathtaking

# A QUIET ACHE

lake view that brought him peace.

As he stepped inside, Clara greeted him warmly, her eyes filled with gratitude. "Come in, Ethan," she said gently, leading him into the living room. "My mom's been having a tough day." Ethan smiled gently and nodded, his expression calm and reassuring, as he had a deep understanding of the elderly and the struggles they faced. He hadn't known her mother personally, but he could sense the weight of the years and the lingering sorrow in the house—a heaviness she had shared with him on the phone several times last week.

Clara motioned for Ethan to sit on the couch across from her mother. "Mom," Clara said, her voice calm, "this is Ethan, an old friend of mine. He's a doctor now, you know, and he wanted to come say hello."

Her mother looked up slowly, her eyes scanning Ethan's face with the faintest flicker of recognition, but it faded quickly. Her mother was no longer the woman who ran the restaurants with fiery passion and endless energy; she was a shadow of herself, lost in the fog of dementia and the ache of her own personal grief.

Ethan sat quietly, watching her. He had been trained to notice the smallest of details—the way people moved, the way they looked, the subtle signs of pain or discomfort they tried to hide. As Clara's mother met his gaze, her expression shifted slightly, and for a moment, he saw a glimmer of something that resembled curiosity.

Ethan cleared his throat, offering a soft smile. "I'm happy to meet you, Mrs. Deveroux," he said gently. "Clara told me a lot about you."

Her eyes flickered again, and her hands trembled as she grasped the armrest. "Clara?... Clara?" she murmured, as if she were trying to place the name. "Yes, my mom. My dear, dear mom."

Ethan nodded, understanding the confusion that clouded her thoughts. It was clear that the years of caring for her had taken their toll on her mind. But there was something about her—something in her presence—that commanded a certain reverence. Then Ethan smiled softly, glancing at Clara.

Clara gently sat beside her mother, her hand resting

## With Clara's Mother

lightly on her arm. "Mom... I'm your daughter," she said softly, her voice filled with tenderness. "You're doing okay. This is my friend, Ethan. He's just here to visit."

There was a long pause, and then Clara's mother turned toward Ethan once more, her eyes searching his face as if trying to decipher his soul. "You... Who?" she asked, her voice soft but tinged with a hint of vulnerability.

Ethan, taken slightly aback by the question, paused for a moment before answering. He could sense the layers of her experiences, the weight of a life filled with both joy and sorrow. With gentle sincerity, he replied slowly, "I am Ethan, your daughter's classmate."

Her mother continued, "Mom, where are you?" Clara gently responded, "Clara here, your daughter, Mom."

Ethan felt a pang of sympathy for her. He could feel the weight of her words—the helplessness, the weariness. He understood all too well the toll that emotional exhaustion could take. His training had prepared him for the physical ailments of people, but moments like these—moments of quiet despair—were something no textbook could teach him to handle.

He knew that dementia was a cruel and relentless disease, stealing memories and fragments of identity bit by bit. But it wasn't just the disease that caused Clara's mother's pain—it was the isolation, the sense of purposelessness that had taken root after the death of her husband. Clara had become her anchor, but even with all her love and devotion, the burden of care was never light; it was a constant weight that pressed down on the heart, both physically and emotionally.

As Ethan sat there, watching Clara gently adjust her mother's pillow on her chest and soothe her with tender words, he couldn't help but feel the deep bond between them. The quiet moments of care, the gentle touch, and the love that radiated from Clara reminded him of the strength and sacrifices she made every hour, every day. She had not only inherited her mother's strength but had cultivated her own, in ways that were perhaps invisible to others. It was a quiet strength, the kind that bore the weight of unspoken fears and quiet sacrifices.

## A QUIET ACHE

Clara's mother, once vibrant and full of life, now seemed lost in the fog of her condition. But in moments like this, Ethan could see the flicker of recognition, the brief glimmer of the woman she had once been. He understood that the work he did, the long hours and exhausting days, were not just about healing bodies—they were about offering people like Clara's mother dignity, even when their minds began to fade.

"Thank you for being here," Clara whispered, breaking his thoughts. "It means more than you know."

The room fell into a silence.

"Mom," Clara whispered, her voice trembling slightly, "Ethan's here with us now. We're not alone in this."

For a brief moment, her mother smiled, the expression fleeting but genuine. It was a smile that spoke of love, of longing for simpler times, of memories that still flickered in the dark recesses of her mind. It was the smile of a woman who had known life in all its beauty and pain—and who still longed for some semblance of peace.

Ethan, though unsure of how much his presence could truly help, felt a quiet determination settle within him. This was more than just a visit; this was a chance to offer comfort, a chance to support the woman who had given so much to Clara. Ethan silently expressed his gratitude to her mother, in his heart, for bringing Clara, such a remarkable person, into the world. He knew the road ahead would be difficult, but he was determined to walk it with Clara—and with her mother—every step of the way.

As noon arrived, the three of them sat together in that big living room—silent but united in the presence of one another. The weight of their shared burdens hung in the air, but so did a quiet, unspoken understanding that no one had to face the darkness alone.

And for that moment, in the presence of her mother, Ethan understood something deep and profound: Even in the midst of sorrow and suffering, there was always room for compassion, tenderness, and the warmth of human connection.

Ethan knew well about dementia, having encountered the

disease in various stages through his years of medical training. In his career, he had cared for many patients suffering from this heartbreaking condition. He had witnessed the many forms it could take—some patients, lost in their confusion, could no longer recognize their spouses, their children, or even their own reflection. The look in their eyes was one of uncertainty, not able to grasp who the people around them were. He had seen others who clung desperately to dolls, as if they were children once again, their small hands gripping the fragile toys with an intensity that no one could break. These patients, trapped in their own memories, wouldn't allow anyone to touch the dolls, as though the inanimate objects were their last remaining link to some semblance of comfort or safety. And now, Clara's mother clutched the pillow tightly to her chest whenever she sat in the chair, a comforting presence that seemed to offer her some sense of security amidst the confusion and disorientation. It was a small but poignant gesture, one that reflected the quiet struggle of her days.

For Ethan, it was always difficult, and he never grew used to it, despite the countless hours spent working with those suffering from dementia. Each case was different, and the emotional toll of watching people lose their identities was something no textbook could prepare him for. But he did know that, at least in those moments, offering comfort, patience, and a steady presence was the best way to help the patient, even if they couldn't fully recognize or understand the kindness being offered.

Deep in thought, he watched Clara carefully helping her mother sip the soup, her gentle hands guiding the spoon to her mother's lips. It struck him that, though he had cared for countless patients in the hospital, this situation felt different. He had helped many patients with similar struggles, offering medications and treatments to ease their symptoms, but he knew that true care went far beyond prescriptions. He had seen time and time again that lifestyle changes, emotional connection, and mental stimulation played just as crucial a role in managing dementia. The idea of doing more than just treating the symptoms was ingrained in him—after all,

# A QUIET ACHE

medication could alleviate pain, but it couldn't restore the lost essence of a person's soul.

He knew the best way to help her mother wouldn't just be through medication. A healthy routine, a rich environment, care with love and positive interactions were essential. He thought of the ways to help her avoid the stagnation that often accompanied dementia—bringing her out of isolation, reintroducing her to familiar places things, or simply taking her out for walks in the fresh air. He also considered the power of familiarity, allowing her to reconnect with old friends or people from the past who could gently remind her of who she once was.

Ethan wasn't sure how to bring this up to Clara, but he could see the weight of her responsibilities. He longed to step in and share the load, to offer ideas and guidance that might help her mother find a sense of joy or purpose again, even if it was fleeting. He knew the road would be long and filled with challenges, but perhaps together, they could find a way to help her mother rediscover some piece of the woman she used to be.

A strange feeling stirred within him as he watched Clara gently tend to her mother. It wasn't like the distant compassion he felt for the patients he treated daily. This was different. Her mother, frail and vulnerable, seemed to radiate a quiet power that tugged at something deep inside him.

He couldn't quite place the feeling—was it admiration? Responsibility? Or perhaps, something even more profound? The thought crept into his mind unbidden, almost startling him: *Is it because I love Clara?*

The realization left him momentarily still, as if the weight of it needed time to settle. He glanced at Clara, her face tender and strong despite the burden she carried. In that moment, Ethan understood that this wasn't just about caring for her mother—it was about standing by Clara, becoming the support she had been longing for.

He sat quietly, observing her mother as she finished her soup, his mind working through the best way to approach the situation. He knew the importance of not overwhelming someone with dementia, which was why he kept his posture open and relaxed. He'd learned through experience that crossing one's arms or standing directly in front of a person with dementia could inadvertently create a sense of distance or discomfort. It was all about creating a calm and safe space for them to feel as at ease as possible.

People with dementia often struggled with confusion and anxiety, sometimes losing track of time or becoming distressed by things they couldn't understand. They might find it difficult to differentiate between what was real and what was a distant memory or a completely imagined event. Ethan had seen patients who would recall past events as though they were happening right then, or worse, who would seem to lose touch with their identity entirely. Understanding this, he approached her mother with a gentle and compassionate demeanor.

When the last spoonful of soup was finished, he looked up at Clara, who was still tending to her mother with care. He knew this was the moment to gently suggest a change in approach. "Clara," he began softly, "one thing I've found in my work is that a good part of dementia care isn't just about managing symptoms with medication—it's also about offering new experiences and making life as rich as possible. Your mom needs to stay connected to the world around her, even if that means small changes."

Clara looked at him with a mixture of curiosity and exhaustion, grateful yet uncertain. "What do you mean?"

Ethan smiled, sensing her openness. "It's important to take her out when you can, even for short walks. The change of scenery, the fresh air, meeting new people, even briefly, can help her mind stay engaged. Maybe visit places she used to love, or just take a stroll through the park. It'll provide a sense of normalcy and prevent the isolation that so often worsens the symptoms."

Clara paused, her eyes softening with a touch of relief. She hadn't thought of it that way, but it made so much sense. "I never considered that... It's been so hard to balance everything. I just wanted her to be comfortable."

Ethan placed a reassuring hand on her shoulder, offering a genuine smile. "I know, and it's not easy. But what your

## A QUIET ACHE

mom really needs now is to reconnect with life, not just through routine, but through moments of joy. Even if it's just a brief outing, something different can help her feel a sense of belonging, of being part of the world again."

Clara's eyes welled up slightly, her heart touched by his kindness and understanding. She had always been a caretaker, but hearing this from someone who understood the depth of her mother's condition, someone who had been through it with countless other patients, gave her a renewed sense of hope. She nodded, grateful for the suggestion, and for the first time in a while, she felt like she had a direction to move forward.

"Thank you so much," she whispered, her voice full of emotion.

Ethan simply nodded, understanding the weight she carried. "You're not alone. I'm here."

Clara looked at him with a warm heart, her gaze filled with gratitude and something deeper. Without saying a word, she reached out and hugged him tightly. The embrace wasn't just one of thanks; it was something more, something that conveyed the silent strength she had found in him—a strength she hadn't felt in a long time. After the painful and lonely years following her broken marriage, this hug felt like the pillar of support she had been searching for, even if she hadn't realized it until now.

Ethan stood still for a moment, taken aback by the intensity of the hug. It wasn't just a gesture of gratitude—it was a deep, unspoken connection. He could feel the weight of her sorrow and the relief of finding someone who understood, someone who could provide the kind of support she hadn't dared to expect. But there was something else, too. In her arms, he felt the quiet trembling of vulnerability, the raw emotion of a woman who had faced so much alone and was now letting someone in.

For Clara, the embrace was a release. For the first time in a long while, she allowed herself to lean on someone else, to feel what it was like to not carry all the burdens alone. Ethan, who had always been a quiet presence in her life, was now the one who stood firm in her storm. And for Ethan, the hug was more than a simple gesture of kindness—it was a reminder of the impact his presence had on others. It was a reminder that sometimes, the quietest support can hold the greatest power.

They pulled away slowly, the moment lingering in the air between them. Neither spoke right away, both processing what had just passed between them. The silence was comfortable, filled with a shared understanding. Ethan gave Clara a soft smile, his hand resting gently on her shoulder.

"You don't have to carry everything alone," he said quietly, his voice sincere. "You're not alone in this, from now on."

Clara nodded, a tear slipping down her cheek, though she smiled back at him with a strength she hadn't known she still had. "Thank you. For everything."

And in that quiet moment, something shifted between them—an unspoken bond formed, a connection that had been growing quietly but steadily. Both knew that the future held uncertainties, but for the first time in a long while, Clara felt like she wasn't facing it alone.

"Honey, pee..." her mother's voice suddenly broke the sacred moment between the two, shattering the quiet connection that hung in the air. Clara gave a small, apologetic smile. "My mom's calling me," she said softly. "She used to call my dad 'honey' all the time, so now she calls everyone the same."

Clara stood up and hurried over to her mother, only to find her sitting there, looking around with a puzzled expression. "What is it, Mom? Do you need to go?" she asked gently, crouching beside her.

Her mother shook her head slowly, her frail hands reaching out for the pillow that had just fallen to the floor. "Give it to me," she murmured, her voice tinged with childlike longing. Clara chuckled softly, a mixture of love and weariness in her eyes. She grabbed the familiar pillow her mother always clung to and placed it in her arms.

As her mother hugged the pillow tightly, a look of comfort and peace washed over her face. Clara returned to Ethan, smiling faintly. "She always wants that pillow. It's like her little anchor," she explained, her voice tinged with

# A QUIET ACHE

bittersweet tenderness. Ethan nodded, his admiration for Clara deepening.

"Now, let's go, Clara," He said suddenly, his voice firm but calm.

"What do you mean?" She asked, caught off guard by his abrupt suggestion.

"We're taking her outside for a bit," Ethan replied with a reassuring nod.

Clara blinked in surprise, then a look of realization crossed her face. "Oh... I see," she murmured. "Now?"

Ethan nodded again, already moving to help. "Yes, now. Fresh air will do her good. Trust me."

Without another word, he gently but efficiently helped Clara prepare her mother. Together, they placed her in the wheelchair, wrapping a light blanket around her legs to shield her from the cool breeze.

As they stepped out of the house, Clara glanced at Ethan, her heart brimming with gratitude and something deeper she couldn't quite name. For the first time in a long while, she felt like she wasn't carrying the weight of her world alone.

Before heading out, Ethan gently placed a hand on Clara's shoulder and said, "Stay close to her. Be by her side so she knows you're there. I'll walk a few feet ahead of her—not too far—just enough so she doesn't feel overwhelmed or scared outside. It's important that she senses both safety and direction: you for reassurance, and me as a guide, someone leading the way and protecting her."

Clara looked at him, her eyes filled with trust. She nodded without hesitation. "Alright," she said softly. "I'll do whatever you suggest. I know you understand these things better than anyone."

Ethan offered a small smile before taking his position. Clara gently took her mother's hand, ensuring she felt comforted, while Ethan walked ahead, leading the way with calm confidence. Together, they moved as a team, each step filled with care and purpose.

As they stepped out of the house, Clara's mother suddenly began to cry loudly, her frail body trembling with fear and confusion. The unexpected outburst startled Clara, and she turned to Ethan with wide, anxious eyes, her voice trembling. "What's wrong, Ethan? Why is she crying?" For a moment, she looked like a little girl seeking comfort and guidance, unsure of what to do.

Ethan, staying calm, gently placed his hand on Clara's shoulder. "Don't worry," he said in a steady voice. "It's normal with this condition. It's something called pseudobulbar affect, or PBA. People with PBA can laugh or cry suddenly and uncontrollably, even if they don't actually feel that way. It's just the way their brain processes emotions." Clara, though still concerned, nodded and took a deep breath, trusting his knowledge. "So... what should we do now?" she asked softly.

"It's important we don't rush her. Let's stay patient and calm," Ethan reassured her. "She'll settle down in time."

Clara nodded, her initial panic giving way to cautious determination. As she adjusted her pace and spoke gently to her mother, Ethan recalled Filipe's words from years ago, spoken as they stood together at Pine Mountain: *"Life's struggles might feel like mountains, but you climb them one step at a time."* Those words, simple yet profound, had stayed with Ethan and now echoed in his mind as he guided Clara and her mother through this delicate moment.

Clara glanced at Ethan, her eyes filled with gratitude, as she held her mother's hand tightly, drawing strength from his steady presence. Together, they continued, moving forward slowly, allowing time and compassion to ease the way.

Her mother's cries were heart-wrenching, but she trusted his expertise.

Ethan knelt down in front of Clara's mother, his voice calm and soothing. "It's okay, ma'am. We're just taking a little trip outside. You're safe."

The mother's sobs quieted a little, though tears still glistened in her eyes. Clara watched in awe as Ethan's calm demeanor seemed to reach her mother. He didn't rush; he didn't force. Instead, he waited patiently for her mother to feel more at ease.

Together, they walked slowly down the garden path. Clara's mother held tightly to a pillow she'd insisted on

# A QUIET ACHE

bringing, her trembling hands clutching it like a lifeline. Each step felt monumental, but with Ethan's steady guidance and Clara's loving presence, they moved forward.

As they reached the corner of the garden, a soft breeze rustled through the trees, carrying the scent of blooming flowers. Ethan stopped and turned back to Clara and her mother. "Let's sit here for a while," he suggested, pointing to a small bench under the shade of a tree. Clara nodded, helping her mother settle into a comfortable spot.

The older woman's expression softened as she looked around, her hands still clutching the pillow. For a moment, her gaze seemed to clear, and she looked at Clara. "It's... beautiful," she murmured, her voice faint but sincere.

Clara smiled, tears pricking her eyes. She hadn't heard her mother speak with such clarity in a long time. Ethan sat nearby, watching quietly, giving them space but staying close enough to help if needed.

After a few minutes of silence, Clara turned to Ethan. "I don't know how to thank you," she said, her voice trembling with emotion. "You've done more for us in one afternoon than I've managed in months."

He shook his head gently, his gaze soft but steady. "You've been doing so much. The love and care you give her—it's not something everyone can manage."

Ethan paused, glancing out the window where the afternoon sun filtered through the trees. "Remember, it's not just about keeping her comfortable at home. Every day, you should take her out into nature—fresh air, trees, sunlight... Let her feel alive, even in the smallest ways. Don't keep her cooped up inside the house for too long. She needs more than just walls around her—she needs to feel the world outside, to feel free."

Clara's eyes softened, gratitude and resolve shining in them. She reached out to gently touch Ethan's arm. "Thank you. I needed to hear that."

Ethan smiled, his voice quiet but firm. "You're not alone in this. And don't forget to take care of yourself, too. She needs you strong and well."

Clara nodded with trust, her voice steady as she replied,

"Yes, I will. Thank you." She looked at him, her heart swelling with gratitude. In that moment, she saw him not just as a friend from her past but as someone who had stepped into her life with kindness and strength, someone who was willing to share her burdens.

As they headed home and sat outside, facing the lakeview—Ethan, Clara, and her mother—shared a quiet moment of peace. For the first time in a long while, Clara felt a glimmer of joy and hope. She didn't have to face this journey alone anymore.

\*\*\*

After a long week tending to patients at the hospital, Ethan decided to dedicate his Saturdays to helping Clara and her mother. And with his parents, Ethan visited them often, especially on Sundays when he would spend the entire day to staying with them. These Sundays became cherished moments of rest and connection, where he would help his parents with household tasks, cook meals together, and share heartfelt conversations over the dining table. His days were often packed with responsibilities and loving care, but his unwavering commitment to family and service brought him a profound sense of purpose and joy.

Ethan found himself visiting Clara more often now. Whether it was to lend a hand with her mother's care, to sit by the window overlooking the serene lake, or simply to offer her a kind ear and quiet company, his presence became a steady part of her days. His visits brought a sense of comfort and encouragement that Clara hadn't realized she needed as before, and each time he left, he seemed to leave behind a warmth that lingered long after.

No matter how exhausting his week at the hospital had been, Saturdays with Clara were sacred. He found deep joy and meaning in their shared work, whether it was tending to the garden, helping with household repairs, or simply sitting together in quiet prayer and reflection. These Saturdays were not just about offering his help—they were moments that rejuvenated his spirit, strengthened his bonds with Clara and her mother.

More importantly, he wanted to see Clara—to hear her

# A QUIET ACHE

voice, to catch the light in her eyes when she spoke about something that mattered to her. Each visit wasn't just about lending a hand; it was a chance to be close to her, to share in the quiet moments that had become unexpectedly meaningful.

***

"Let's take her to the shopping mall," Ethan suggested casually, catching Clara off guard.

"The mall?" Clara repeated, her brow furrowed in surprise. "Are you sure that's a good idea?"

Ethan smiled reassuringly. "It'll be good for her. Familiar places or environments with a variety of sights and sounds can sometimes help bring a spark of joy or even nostalgia. Plus, it gives her the chance to feel a part of life outside the house."

With a mix of curiosity and trust, Clara agreed. Once they reached the mall, Ethan leaned closer to her and whispered, "Ask her what she'd like to do. Even small choices can make her feel more in control and engaged."

Clara hesitated for a moment before kneeling beside her mother's wheelchair. She leaned in close, her voice soft and full of care. "Mom, we're at the mall. Do you like it here? Is there something you'd like to do? Something you want to see? Or maybe you can get something you like?"

Ethan gently touched her shoulder and added in a calm tone, "Clara, keep it simple. Use short sentences and repeat them a few times—give her mind a chance to process."

Clara nodded, taking his advice to heart. She turned back to her mother, her tone now slower and more deliberate. "Mom, maybe something here you want to see?"

Her mother's eyes flickered with recognition as she slowly looked around, the repetition helping to ground her in the moment. "I... scarves," she murmured softly, her voice trembling with a mix of uncertainty and eagerness.

Clara smiled warmly, her heart swelling at the rare moment of clarity. "Alright, Mom. Let's go there."

Ethan pushed the wheelchair while Clara walked alongside, holding her mother's hand. They stopped at a colorful display of scarves, and her mother's eyes lit up as she reached out to touch the soft fabrics.

"That one," she said, pointing to a deep blue scarf with delicate floral embroidery.

Clara picked it up and draped it gently over her mother's shoulders. "It looks beautiful on you, Mom," she said with genuine affection.

Ethan watched the exchange with a quiet smile, feeling a deep sense of fulfillment. Moments like these reminded him why he had chosen this path in life. As they continued through the mall, stopping to explore small shops and even grabbing ice cream, he noticed how Clara's mother seemed to relax and smile more.

\*\*\*

When they returned home later that afternoon, Clara turned to Ethan with gratitude shining in her eyes. "I haven't seen her this engaged in... so long."

Ethan shrugged modestly. "Sometimes, it's the little things that make the biggest difference."

Clara looked at him for a long moment, her voice soft. "It's not just the little things. It's you, Ethan."

The warmth in her voice and the moment they shared hung in the air as they both turned their attention back to her mother. "You've been a constant, steady presence... in a way I never expected, but needed more than I could've realized. You're not just a friend. You've been... my strength, even when I didn't know how to find my own," she said gently.

Ethan gazed at her, his heart softening as he absorbed the weakness in her words. Gently, yet with a steady conviction, he said, "you're doing everything you can, and that's enough. I'm here, every step of the way."

She looked up at him, her eyes reflecting a quiet closeness, yet filled with peace. "I know," she said softly, her voice carrying the weight of her thoughts. "But there are times when it still feels overwhelming."

He sat down beside her, offering a full presence. "It's okay to feel overwhelmed. But remember, every small step you take makes a difference, that's something to be proud of." Clara smiled faintly, her hand reaching to clasp Ethan's. "Thank you for reminding me. I think... I think I've been so

# A QUIET ACHE

focused on what I couldn't fix, I forgot to see what I *could* do."

Ethan squeezed her hand gently. "That's the key. Focus on what you can do. The rest will follow."

The room was peaceful, the soft sound of Clara's mother humming softly to herself in the background as she adjusted the scarf around her neck.

"One step at a time," she whispered to herself, remembering Ethan's words. She looked over at him, her expression softening. "One step at a time."

Ethan gave a small nod, his gaze steady on her. "Exactly," he said quietly. "One step at a time."

***

As usual, another Saturday arrived, but this time, things were different. Ethan suggested a visit to one of the restaurants that had once belonged to Clara's family. It was the place her mother had poured her heart and soul into before dementia had taken much of her memory. The idea of returning to a place so familiar brought a sense of nostalgia, but also a hint of uncertainty.

Clara hesitated for a moment, unsure of how her mother would react. But Ethan's encouraging smile and calm demeanor gave her the strength to move forward. They carefully helped her mother into the car and set off toward the restaurant.

When they arrived, the moment they stepped inside, her mother's eyes widened in surprise. She seemed confused at first, but as they approached the familiar counters and the soft hum of the kitchen, something stirred in her. The walls were lined with pictures from her past, menus from old events, and the gentle chatter of people enjoying their meals.

Her mother's face softened as she looked around, her eyes lighting up with recognition. She seemed to stand taller in her seat, her gaze moving from one corner of the restaurant to another, as if she were revisiting old memories that had long been hidden. "It's... it's mine," she whispered softly, her voice trembling with emotion. "Clara! This was mine... we did this, Clara, didn't we?"

Clara, holding her mother's hand, nodded gently. "Yes,

Mom. It's ours. It's always been yours." Her heart skipped a beat when her mother softly spoke her name, a name that had been so often lost in the haze of her dementia. It was as if time had stood still for a moment. Clara's eyes welled with tears, but she smiled warmly, holding her mother's hand tightly. She felt a rush of tenderness for her mother and a deep sense of gratitude for Ethan's idea to bring them here.

"Clara..." Her mother repeated, her voice trembling but steady, as though she were reclaiming a part of herself. "I... I love you, my dear."

Clara's chest tightened with emotion. After all these years, after the countless moments of confusion, fear, and frustration, hearing her mother say her name felt like a gift—a brief but precious connection that made all the trials worth it. She leaned in, her voice gentle and loving. "I love you too, Mom. I've always been here, and I'll always be here."

Her mother smiled faintly, a distant look in her eyes, but there was a sense of recognition there, a soft acknowledgment of the bond between them that had never truly faded. Clara could feel a sense of peace settle over her, a quiet relief that her mother still knew her in some deep, unspoken way.

The brief moment of clarity was like a light shining through the fog of dementia. Clara felt incredibly grateful for it, even if it was fleeting. It reminded her that love, in its purest form, was always present—sometimes hidden, but always there beneath the surface.

Ethan, watching from the side, could see the change in Clara's expression. He didn't speak, but there was something deeply moving about the scene. It was a simple moment, yet one filled with so much meaning. The small victories—like remembering a name—were what mattered most in times like this. And for Clara, it was a moment she would cherish forever.

Her mother's voice brought Clara back to the present. "I love you, dear daughter," she said, her hand weakly patting Clara's.

Clara blinked back the tears, her heart full. "I love you, Mom."

## A QUIET ACHE

The evening continued in a quiet, peaceful rhythm. The once-bustling restaurant, now less familiar to her mother, felt like a gentle reminder of the past. Clara could sense her mother's joy in the familiarity of the place, even though it was no longer hers in the way it once had been. But for tonight, it didn't matter. Tonight, her mother had connected with something that felt like home.

Ethan stood by, watching them quietly, his presence a steady support, allowing her and her mother to experience this moment in their own way. He had witnessed firsthand the immense challenge she faced in caring for her mother, how many days she had borne the weight of both love and exhaustion, all while disregarding her own youth and needs. It was as if her own well-being had become secondary to the endless devotion she gave, yet he could see how much it had drained her spirit over time.

Seeing this small, beautiful moment between them filled him with a quiet sense of pride.

Ethan, with his expertise in dementia and aging, understood the complexities of Clara's mother's condition. Here was a woman whose mind had begun to fade, yet her love still lingered in the small, tender gestures she offered. Even as her memories blurred and slipped away, Ethan could see how deeply rooted her affection for Clara was. It was as if love had its own kind of permanence, transcending the mind's limitations. Though words were often lost, the warmth in her touch, the way her eyes would soften when Clara was near, spoke volumes. Ethan had come to realize that love, in its truest form, remained even when everything else faded. He understood now that even in her confusion, there was a deep reservoir of care and warmth. She had given Clara life, and in some way, she had given him a deeper understanding of the fragility and resilience of the human spirit. In every quiet smile and every moment of connection, Ethan saw that love had no boundaries, no limits. It could transcend the mind, the body, and time itself.

When the meal ended, and Clara's mother had grown sleepy, Clara gently guided her back to the car. Ethan offered a hand to her mother to steady her as they made their way

## With Clara's Mother

outside, his usual professional composure softened by the warmth of the evening.

On the way home, Clara sat in the back with her mother, whispering softly to her and helping her settle. Ethan drove, his eyes occasionally glancing in the rearview mirror to check on them. The ride was quiet, but it was the kind of silence that felt comfortable, as if the simple act of being together, without words, was enough.

When they arrived at the house, Ethan helped Clara bring her mother inside and settle her into her favorite chair. It wasn't long before her mother was gently dozing off, the exhaustion of the day catching up to her. Clara kissed her forehead softly and sat beside her, taking a deep breath, her hands resting on her mother's.

Ethan watched them for a moment before quietly excusing himself. He knew that this wasn't just another Saturday for Clara. It had been a day filled with small, significant victories. He could see how the small moments of clarity with her mother meant so much. Before leaving, he looked at Clara, his gaze filled with understanding.

"You're doing more than you realize," he said softly, his voice filled with a quiet sincerity. "What you're doing for her—it matters."

Clara nodded, wiping away a stray tear that had escaped down her cheek. "I just want her to remember me," she whispered. "Even if just for a little while."

Ethan smiled gently. "She does. She does."

With that, he turned to leave, but not before casting one last glance at the woman who had raised Clara—her mother, the woman who had once been full of life.

As the door closed behind him, Clara sat in the quiet of her living room, surrounded by the presence of her mother. There was peace in her heart, knowing that they had shared a moment—a brief but precious one—and that, despite the challenges, they would continue to find ways to connect, even if it was only for a fleeting second.

And in that silence, Clara understood: Love had the power to transcend the boundaries of memory. Despite her mother's fragile state, the bond they shared remained unbroken, a love that was not bound by time or sight but by something far deeper—a connection that would never fade, even when the world seemed to grow dim. Clara felt her mother's presence in her heart, a hidden strength that would guide her forward.

***

That night, Clara couldn't sleep. She tossed and turned, her mind restless, consumed by thoughts of Ethan. From the time they were in high school, when she had barely noticed him, to now, with all the unwavering support he had shown her and her mother. She reflected on the moments she had overlooked or taken for granted. Since their unexpected encounter at the park, she had come to realize just how much Ethan had quietly been there for her, offering more than just his expertise—he had been offering his sincere heart. In subtle gestures and unspoken support, he had shown her that she wasn't alone in her struggles, and that his care went far beyond mere duty. Each moment spent together, each word of encouragement, had gently woven a deeper bond between them, one grounded in trust and understanding.

She hadn't seen it before, but now it was clear—he had been a steady presence all along, and perhaps, in the most unexpected way, he had always been the one to help her heal.

# CHAPTER FIVE
# Through Tears

One Sunday morning, Ethan invited Clara to a local coffee shop for a much-needed break. She hesitated for a moment. Then, she asked her neighbor to look after her mother for a few hours. It was a rare chance to step away from the weight of caregiving.

At the coffee shop, Clara found herself feeling refreshed and at ease. It had been such a long time since she had taken a moment like this—just to sit, relax, and feel the world move around her. Her life had been consumed by caring for her ailing mother and retreating into herself after the pain of her broken marriage. But now, sitting across from Ethan, something shifted. She felt an unfamiliar sense of safety and peace, as though the walls she had built around her heart were beginning to soften.

She shared about her life after high school, how she had gone from the dreams of youth to a marriage she never truly wanted.

Her voice softened as she spoke about her father's sudden accident, a pivotal moment in her life that had altered everything. Clara's voice trembled as she spoke, the weight of memories pressing down on her. She had never shared the full story with anyone before, but something about Ethan's quiet understanding made her feel safe enough to open up.

"Before my father's accident, he wanted me to marry his colleague, a man named Corad, who originated from Germany." She began, her gaze fixed on the floor as if reliving the pain. "He was younger than my father, but twelve years older than me. I never truly loved him, but... I thought it was what my parents wanted, and I had to do it to please them."

"After my father passed away," she said quietly, "I felt lost. The way my marriage unfolded... it all felt so scary, so empty." She took a deep breath before continuing, "It wasn't the life I had imagined."

Ethan remained silent, allowing her the space to speak,

# A QUIET ACHE

knowing how difficult it was to revisit such painful parts of her past. Clara continued, her voice quieter now. "He was never who I thought he was. At first, I didn't see it. But over time, things began to change. After my father's death, Corad became more violent and unpredictable, as if there was no one to hold him in check. He was never lacking money as a lawyer, but why? He was involved in things... things I couldn't even comprehend at the time. He was caught dealing drugs, and his whole world seemed to crumble. He wanted me to support him in his illegal business, but he never told me exactly what he was doing. I just felt something was wrong, so I refused to cooperate with him."

"I'm glad you trusted your instincts. It's not easy, but you did the right thing." Ethan said softly.

Clara continued, "I didn't want to get involved, but it was hard. He kept pressuring me, but I knew I had to stay away from it. In the end, he was arrested and sentenced to 19 years in jail. However, he got into fights with other inmates while there and was tragically killed." Sadly, she continued, "he was not a simple man, you know. He beat me almost every single day. He hated me for reasons I couldn't understand. Maybe it was because I wasn't the person he wanted. Maybe it was because I was too weak to stand up to him," she spoke softly, her words laced with a quiet pain as she mentioned Corad. "He didn't want children," she said, her voice steady but carrying a deep sadness. "He told me he didn't like children. Over time, I realized... he didn't see me as a wife, but more as something to control and manipulate... He used me—treated me like a toy, violently at times. It was as though I didn't matter beyond what he wanted from me." Her eyes grew distant as she recounted the memories, the weight of those years still pressing on her heart.

Clara swallowed her tears, her throat tightening as she fought to hold back the emotions that threatened to spill over. She fell silent for a moment, her gaze fixed on the floor as she gathered her thoughts, the quiet stretching between them. The weight of her words seemed to stay in the air, heavy and raw, as she composed herself before speaking again. "I stayed because I thought it was my duty. I thought I

*Through Tears*

had to fix things, make him better, but it only got worse. I felt smaller, more invisible to him. He made me believe that it was all my fault, that I was the problem and a barrier to his business."

Ethan's heart ached for her as he listened, knowing the pain she had carried all these years, silently. He reached out to her, his hand resting gently on hers.

"You didn't deserve that," he said, his voice filled with compassion. "You didn't deserve any of it."

Clara let out a shaky breath, a small nod. "I know, now. But at the time, I didn't know how to leave him. I felt trapped, as if I had no way out. He had a way of making me feel small, of making me feel like I had no options. I didn't know where to go, and I didn't want to disappoint my mother, especially since she wasn't well."

Clara sighed deeply, her voice heavy with the weight of the past. "When he was in jail, the house we lived in was seized by the government. Now, I'm back at my parents' house, trying to start over and to look after my mom."

Ethan, with a look of understanding, replied, "I can't imagine how difficult that must have been for you. But you're strong, and you're making it through." Clara gave a small, bittersweet smile. "It's been hard, but I have to keep going, for my mother, for myself..."

Ethan squeezed her hand gently, offering her the quiet support that she so often gave to others. "I can't imagine how difficult that must have been," he said. "But you're free from him now. And you're not alone. You don't have to carry that burden anymore."

Clara smiled faintly, looking at him with gratitude in her eyes. "I've been carrying it for so long. But talking about it... it helps. It helps more than I thought it would."

The weight of the past still lingered between them, but in that moment, there was a sense of relief—a sense that, little by little, she was finding a way to heal, to let go of the scars that had shaped her.

Ethan stayed silent, simply being there with her, offering a comfort that words alone couldn't provide.

In the end, she admitted softly, her voice tinged with

vulnerability, "I don't know why I'm sharing all of this with you. It's just... everything seems to spill out when I talk to you, and I'm sorry if I've caused you any concern." She looked down, her fingers nervously tracing the edge of her coffee cup. Ethan leaned forward, his gaze steady and reassuring as he replied, "don't apologize. I'm grateful that you trust me enough to share these things. Sometimes, keeping it all inside makes the weight unbearable. Letting it out, even just a little, can bring relief. And if sharing with me helps, even in the smallest way, I'm here." His words were calm yet deeply empathetic, and for the first time in a long while, she felt a warmth—a sense of safety and understanding she hadn't experienced in years.

Her heart was now dancing, even as she shared the saddest parts of her life. She couldn't quite understand why she dared to open up so easily to a man—even though he had been a former classmate. There was something inexplicably different about Ethan. It felt strange, yet comforting, as if her heart had already decided something her mind couldn't yet grasp. This man, sitting across from her with his steady gaze and understanding words, seemed to see right through her fears and pain. It was as though he instinctively knew what she needed—not just advice or sympathy, but a genuine connection and a quiet strength she hadn't realized she'd been longing for.

As for Ethan, he could feel his heart becoming ever more connected to her. Every painful word she shared clung deeply to his heart, resonating with a tenderness he hadn't felt in years. Clara was different now—mature and thoughtful, shaped by the struggles she had endured. She no longer carried the carefree joy of their high school days, but there was something about her, something profound and quietly resilient, that drew him in even more. It wasn't just her story that captivated him; it was the depth of her character, the strength in her vulnerability, and the quiet grace with which she faced the weight of her past. To him, she was someone who awakened something deep and enduring within him.

Then Ethan said, his voice gentle but firm, "Can we go somewhere quiet, for some fresh air?"

*Through Tears*

Clara nodded, sensing his need for some space to share or reflect, and together they stood up. They left the coffee shop and walked down the bustling street, making their way to a small park nearby. The air was cooler here, the noise from the city fading into the background as the tranquility of the park surrounded them. They walked side by side, the quiet of the space offering a comfortable stillness, allowing them both to breathe more easily. The park, with its calm paths and shaded trees, felt like a perfect place to pause and continue their conversation, away from the world's distractions.

Hand in hand with Ethan, walking outside, Clara felt a shift within herself.

Out of nowhere, she felt a sharp stinging sensation in her head, something she occasionally experienced. She raised her hand to press gently on her forehead, hoping to ease the pain.

Ethan noticed it immediately and asked, "Are you okay, Clara?"

She replied with a faint smile, her voice soft but reassuring, "I am fine." Her words, though simple, carried a sense of calm, as if she were trying to convince herself as much as Ethan.

The sky above seemed to open up, clearer and more beautiful than she had ever noticed before. The surrounding landscape, once ordinary, now appeared profoundly peaceful, as if the world had transformed into something softer, more serene. It was as if the weight of her words had lightened the air, allowing her to see everything around her in a new light—a moment of clarity, of stillness, in the midst of everything she'd been carrying.

Finding a quiet spot, they sat down together on the soft grass beneath a towering old red oak tree. The serene environment seemed to offer them both a moment of peace. After a few moments of silence, Ethan spoke softly, his voice calm yet filled with understanding.

"Clara," he began slowly, "your ex-husband... he's wounded. I can see it in so many people, really. Having more money, they always want more. But it's never really about the money. It's about something deeper inside them, something empty they can't quite fill, no matter how much they

# A QUIET ACHE

accumulate. They don't know what to do with that emptiness, or where to go. They thought they could fill that emptiness, but little did they know, they only deepened it further."

His words hung in the air between them, and Clara listened closely, her mind processing the depth of what he was saying. She had never thought of her ex-husband in that way, but the truth in his voice resonated with her, and she felt a shift in her understanding of the past.

Clara sat in quiet contemplation, her fingers lightly grazing the grass beneath her. Ethan's words, so gentle yet piercing, had a way of unlocking thoughts she hadn't fully confronted before. She had spent so much of her life trying to make sense of the turmoil with her ex-husband, blaming herself, and at times even feeling lost in her own anger and sadness. But what he had said opened a new door of understanding.

She looked at him, her eyes searching for something, maybe for the same reassurance he had always given her in those small moments of vulnerability. "I never thought of it like that," she whispered, her voice barely audible in the quiet afternoon. "I always thought it was just him... But maybe... maybe it was his emptiness. That constant hunger for more, no matter the cost. I always wondered what drove him."

Ethan turned slightly, meeting her gaze, his expression gentle but resolute. "People like that," he said, "they're always searching for something, but they don't know what. They try to fill that void with possessions, control, even people. But no matter how much they gain, they can't fill it up because the emptiness comes from within. It's something they have to face—if they can."

Clara nodded slowly, feeling the weight of his words settle within her. "I think I've spent so much time trying to fix him, trying to understand what went wrong," she said, a sad smile forming on her lips. "But maybe the truth is, I can't fix him. No one can. He has to find his own way out of that darkness."

Ethan placed a reassuring hand on her shoulder, his touch grounding her. "You can't fix someone else's pain. You can only walk beside them if they want you there. And if they don't... it's okay. You deserve peace too."

The quiet hum of the afternoon surrounded them, the gentle rustle of leaves above a soft soundtrack to their conversation. Clara let out a breath she didn't realize she'd been holding. The weight on her shoulders seemed much lighter, as if some invisible burden had been lifted, even just for a moment. She wasn't sure where her journey would lead from here, but in a long while, she felt a glimmer of happiness.

"Thank you so much," she said softly, her voice filled with gratitude. "You've given me something to think about. Something I think I needed to hear."

Ethan smiled warmly, his eyes reflecting sincerity. "You don't have to thank me. I'm just glad I can be here for you. And I'll always be here."

Clara felt a warmth spread through her chest, a tenderness she hadn't allowed herself to feel in years. She had been so used to carrying everything on her own, so accustomed to building walls around her heart to protect it from the pain. But sitting there with Ethan, the walls felt less necessary. There was a quiet safety in his presence.

For a moment, the world around them seemed to fade away, leaving only the two of them sitting beneath the sprawling tree, surrounded by the peace of the park. The bustle of the city seemed distant, muffled by the stillness of the afternoon.

"I didn't know I needed this," she whispered, her voice barely more than a breath. "I didn't realize how much I've been holding onto."

Ethan nodded, his expression soft but understanding. "It's okay to let go sometimes. You've been through so much. Everything will be fine. You deserve to breathe, to feel lighter."

She closed her eyes for a moment, letting the words settle in. She had spent so long focusing on what she had lost—her marriage, the sense of security, the dreams she once had. But perhaps, just perhaps, there was something still worth holding onto: herself. And maybe even a chance to rebuild, to heal, and to open her heart again.

# A QUIET ACHE

When she opened her eyes, she found Ethan watching her, his gaze gentle and sincere. There was a strength in his presence that made her feel as though, no matter what happened, she would be okay.

"Ethan," she began, her voice stronger now, "thank you for helping me see things differently. I don't know what the future holds, but I know I don't have to face it alone. And I'm not as afraid as I used to be."

He smiled, his heart swelling with something unspoken. "You don't have to be afraid. Whatever comes, we'll figure it out. Together."

Her heart fluttered at his words, the simple promise of support and understanding wrapping around her like a comforting blanket. She didn't know what would happen next, or how the road ahead would unfold. But now she felt a sense of peace that she hadn't known in years. With Ethan by her side, maybe, just maybe, she could start to believe in a future that wasn't defined by her past.

As they sat in silence, the sun shining from high, casting a warm, golden glow across the landscape. She allowed herself a small smile. She wasn't sure what was ahead, but she was finally ready to take it one step at a time.

As the conversation came to a natural pause, she glanced at the sky, noticing the sun.

She knew she couldn't stay out much longer. Her responsibilities at home called her back, her mother's needs constant and unrelenting. It was hard for Clara to step away from the peace she'd found in this moment, but she knew her place was with her mother.

"Oh! I should go now," she said, her voice tinged with reluctance. "I can't stay out too long... my mom... she'll need me." The words sounded heavier than usual, the weight of her caregiving always pressing down on her.

Ethan looked at her with understanding, his expression warm but filled with a quiet sadness. "I know," he said softly, "I don't want you to go now, but I understand. You're doing everything you can for her. You're amazing. Thank you for today."

She gave a small smile, appreciating his words more than

# Through Tears

he knew. She stood up slowly, stretching her legs after sitting for so long.

"I'll walk you to your car," he offered, standing up as well, offering a steady hand to guide her.

They walked side by side, hand in hand, in comfortable silence, the sound of their footsteps the only noise between them. The walk was slow, as though neither wanted to break the calm that had settled over them. When they reached her car, she turned to Ethan, her heart a little heavier, but grateful for the time they had shared.

"Thank you for being with me," she said, her voice soft but sincere. "And for everything. It meant more than I can say."

Ethan smiled, the tenderness in his eyes reflecting the care he felt for her. "I'm just glad I could be here. If you ever need me, you know where to find me." After a few seconds of silence, Ethan said softly, "Clara, could you give me a hug?"

She hesitated for a moment, a hint of shyness in her eyes, but then nodded gently. With that, Ethan pulled her into a tight embrace, his arms wrapping around her with warmth and reassurance, as if to share with her all the strength and hope he had in his heart. A wave of happiness suddenly overwhelmed her. It was an unfamiliar warmth that spread through her, soft and comforting, as if the weight of the world had momentarily lifted. She closed her eyes, letting the feeling wash over her, feeling safe and cared for in Ethan's embrace. It was a simple moment, but it felt like everything she had needed all along.

Clara's heart fluttered.

She didn't know what the future held, but having Ethan by her side, even in moments like these, gave her hope and happiness. She felt less alone, less burdened by the weight of everything she had been carrying for so long. She felt great now.

With a final look into his eyes, she nodded and climbed into her car. "Take care, Ethan," she said, and with a soft wave, she drove off, heading back to her mother's side. But as she drove, she couldn't help but feel a glimmer of

## A QUIET ACHE

something new inside her—a sense of possibility, of connection, that she hadn't allowed herself to feel in a long time. Maybe the future was a little brighter than she had thought.

While walking to his car, Ethan didn't know why, but something strange stirred in his heart. A sense of restlessness began to settle within him, an unfamiliar tension that tugged at him despite their intimate encounter just now. It wasn't fear, but something deeper—something unspoken that seemed to rise with every heartbeat in him. He decided to walk back to the park, his mind swirling with thoughts. The soft rustling of the leaves above him and the distant hum of the city seemed far away, as if the world had paused, just for him. He silently sat down again under the same tree where they had shared their conversation, leaning back against the rough bark.

He thought about how she had opened up to him, sharing the pain she'd been holding in for so long. He hadn't expected her to be so vulnerable, to trust him with such intimate pieces of her life. The ease with which she had shared her hurt, her fears, and her loneliness felt both humbling and heavy. He had always been the one who listened to others, the one who helped, but in that moment, he felt something deeper. He wanted to protect her. He wanted to be there for her in a way that was beyond just offering advice or support.

The thought of Clara caring for her mother, of sacrificing so much for the woman who had raised her, stirred something inside him. He admired her strength, but he also saw how much it was costing her. He understood the kind of exhaustion she must have been feeling, not just physically, but emotionally, as she balanced the weight of her past and the overwhelming responsibility of caring for someone who no longer remembered the world as it was.

His thoughts turned inward. He realized how much he had begun to care for her, more than he ever intended. He didn't want to overthink it, didn't want to rush into something, but he couldn't deny the pull he felt toward her. There was a connection between them, something deeper than he had anticipated.

And yet, Clara's hesitance, her withdrawal, the walls she had built around herself—he understood them. He couldn't just sweep in and erase her past pain, no matter how much he wanted to help. She needed time. She needed space. But he would be there for her, no matter what.

He stood up, taking one last look at the tree, as if drawing strength from the quiet stillness of the moment. He didn't have all the answers, but he knew one thing: He would not let her face this alone. The journey ahead was uncertain, but he was ready to walk beside her, one step at a time.

Now, he also felt uneasy in heart, and decided to take a walk for a couple of hours before heading back home to check on his parents. The air was warm and calming, offering a quiet solace from the bustle of his busy days. As he walked, he noticed the variety of people around him—some leisurely strolling with a sense of purpose, others lost in their thoughts, and still others caught up in conversations that seemed to fill the space with laughter or frustration. The ebb and flow of life continued around him, like a steady current that never stopped.

Eventually, he found himself sitting on a bench in front of a small pond, nestled within the grounds of a government building. The water's surface was calm, reflecting the fading light of the evening sky. People walked past him in pairs, groups, or alone, their lives unfolding in parallel to his own. He watched as children ran past, laughing freely, while others sat on nearby benches, immersed in their phones or chatting with companions.

The contrast between the joy, the sorrow, and the bustle of daily life made him pause. He thought about how modern life had become so fast-paced, so driven by external expectations, that many seemed to have lost sight of the deeper connections that held meaning. People were busy, always rushing somewhere, always looking for the next thing—whether it was the next job, the next relationship, or the next moment of happiness. Yet, as he observed them, he couldn't help but notice the subtle signs of fatigue, of lives that were perhaps a little emptier than they appeared on the surface.

He thought about Clara. She was a perfect example of someone caught in the whirlwind of life, struggling with the weight of her past while trying to care for her mother. She gave so much of herself, yet at times, it seemed as though the world had forgotten her needs. It was a paradox—so much external noise, so much movement, yet so many people, like Clara, carrying invisible burdens that no one could see.

He sighed and leaned back, his thoughts drifting like the clouds above him. Life had a way of forcing people to adapt, to keep moving forward even when the path wasn't clear. But maybe that was the answer, he thought—just keep moving forward, one step at a time. The answers might not come all at once, but as long as you keep walking, eventually, you'll find your way.

As he sat there, feeling the coolness of the air settle over him, he made a silent promise to himself. He would be there for her, to help her through the quiet struggles, to be a presence of stability in her chaotic world. Even if he didn't know all the answers, he knew he could be a part of her journey, one small step at a time.

***

Ethan's heart skipped a beat as he saw Clara's name flash on his phone. He knew something was wrong with Clara. He quickly answered, his voice filled with concern. "Clara, is everything okay?"

Clara's voice was weak, strained with pain as she spoke. "Ethan, I... I don't know. I... have this horrible headache, and I don't feel well... I'm just at home with Mom. I... I don't know what to do." Her words trembled, revealing the depth of her distress, and for a moment, she was silent, her breath shallow and uneven. It was clear that something was wrong, something she couldn't quite explain, and the helplessness in her voice tugged at his heart.

His mind raced. Without hesitation, he stood up from the bench and began running toward the car and drove to her house: "Stay where you are, Clara. I'm on my way."

In the car, he realized that after Clara left him, it was then that the restlessness settled in. The unease lingered, a quiet reminder of something deeper he couldn't yet fully understand or express.

As he arrived at her home 30 minutes later, he could already feel the urgency in his steps. He rushed inside, his eyes scanning the room. Clara was lying down on the couch, her hand pressed to her forehead, her face pale and drawn with discomfort. Her mother was sitting in her wheelchair, looking distant, while a glass of water lay shattered on the floor, the water pooling slowly beneath it.

He knelt beside Clara, gently taking her hand. "Clara, talk to me. What's going on?"

Clara winced, her eyes squeezing shut as she struggled to speak. "It just hit me out of nowhere... My head feels like it's splitting, and I don't know why."

Ethan's medical instincts kicked in, his focus narrowing to the situation. He carefully helped her sit up, his voice calm and reassuring. "I think we need to get you checked out, just to be safe. But first, let me check on your mother."

He turned to her mother, who seemed to be lost in a daze. Then he knelt in front of Clara, checking her vitals quickly. Everything appeared stable, but there was no mistaking the toll that the years of illness had taken on her.

Clara, instinctively sensing something serious, her eyes filled with concern, looked from her mother to Ethan. "What should we do, Ethan? What if it's something serious?"

Ethan gently soothed her, his voice calm and reassuring. "It's okay. We'll take this step by step. First, let's make sure you're comfortable."

He was focused, but inside, his heart ached for her. Seeing her in pain, struggling with the weight of it all, hit him harder than he expected. He couldn't help but feel a deep sense of responsibility—this was more than just a medical emergency for him. It was about being there for her, supporting her in the way she needed most.

He was at her side, calmly. "For now, just rest. Everything will be alright."

Clara closed her eyes, grateful for his calm and steady presence. She could feel the weight of the world lifting, if only a little, knowing Ethan was there to help her through it.

# A QUIET ACHE

And in that moment, she realized just how much Ethan had become a part of her life—someone who wasn't just there when things were easy, but someone who stayed, who cared, and who would stand by her no matter what came next.

Ethan's eyes narrowed as he watched Clara's condition worsen. Her face was pale, and the pain in her eyes was unmistakable. Despite his reassurance moments before, the rapid decline in her condition told him this was not just a simple headache.

He carefully took her hand, his voice calm but urgent. "Clara, I need you to try and stay with me, okay? Just a little longer. I'm going to get you some help right away."

Clara's head leaned back against the couch, her eyes unfocused. Her breathing became shallow, and she could barely manage a whisper, "It's... it's like my head's... about to burst."

Ethan's heart raced. He quickly stood, taking a moment to assess the situation before moving into action. He took out his phone again, calling a nearby hospital for immediate assistance. His hands were steady, but inside, his thoughts were chaotic. He knew the signs, the way her eyes blurred and the intensity of the pain she was feeling—this wasn't something simple. No, it wasn't. This was serious, and it was escalating quickly.

"Listen to me. I'm going to take care of this. Help is on the way," Ethan said, kneeling beside her again, trying to keep her calm. He could feel her pulse racing beneath his touch, the panic beginning to set in.

Clara blinked rapidly, trying to focus on his face, but her vision was fading. "E...than... I... I'm... scared."

Ethan brushed a strand of hair away from her forehead, his expression softening as he spoke with the same steady calm. "I'm right here, Clara. Just breathe. Help will be here in no time. You're not alone."

His heart ached as he watched her struggle to hold onto consciousness. He knew she was strong, but in this moment, he couldn't help but feel helpless. He'd seen his share of medical emergencies, but nothing like this. Not for someone he cared for so deeply.

The seconds felt like hours, but he remained at her side, refusing to leave her alone. Soon, he could hear the faint sound of sirens in the distance—help was on the way. He just hoped it wasn't too late.

As the sirens grew louder, Clara's breathing became more labored. Her fear was palpable, and the pain in her head was only intensifying. Tears welled up in her eyes as she clutched Ethan's hand tightly, her grip desperate and trembling.

"I don't want to die, Ethan," she whispered through ragged breaths, the tears spilling down her cheeks. "Please... I don't want to leave my mother... I can't... I can't leave her alone."

Ethan's heart clenched at her words. He had never seen her this vulnerable, this afraid. His mind raced, but he focused on the one thing that mattered most—getting her the help she so desperately needed. He leaned in closer, his voice gentle yet firm.

"Clara, you're not going anywhere. We're going to make sure of that. You're going to be okay," he said, brushing the tears away from her face as he spoke. His voice was steady, but beneath it, a deep urgency pulsed. He couldn't lose her. Not after everything they had shared, everything he had come to care about.

Clara's sobs deepened, and she buried her face into her hands for a moment. The weight of everything—her past, her mother's illness, and now this overwhelming pain—seemed to crash down on her all at once. She felt completely powerless, as if the world was closing in around her.

Ethan's hand rested on her shoulder, steadying her, offering silent support as she gathered herself. He wasn't sure what would happen next, but one thing was certain: he wasn't going to let her go through this alone.

"I'm right here," he whispered softly, his voice a comforting constant amid the storm of emotions swirling around them. "I'm with you every step of the way. We'll get through this together."

As the ambulance pulled up outside, he helped Clara to her feet, supporting her with gentle care. The paramedics

# A QUIET ACHE

rushed inside, and he explained the situation quickly, his mind still reeling from how quickly things had escalated. Clara's hand was still in his, and despite the chaos, he refused to let it go.

"You're going to be okay," he repeated, his voice soothing despite the whirlwind in his chest. "Just breathe, stay with me. You're not alone."

She nodded faintly, her body weak but her eyes searching his for some semblance of reassurance. He didn't have all the answers, but he knew that in this moment, his presence—his steady, unwavering presence—was the one thing that could help calm her.

As the paramedics moved her onto the stretcher, Ethan stayed by her side. He couldn't bear the thought of her being alone in this moment of fear. He followed closely behind as they loaded her into the ambulance, never letting go of her hand.

The doors of the ambulance closed with a quiet thud, and the vehicle sped away. Ethan's thoughts raced, but all he could focus on was Clara. He would be there with her, no matter what. He would make sure she didn't face this alone.

As the ambulance raced through the streets, Ethan sat beside her, trying to keep his emotions in check. His mind was swirling, but his thoughts were laser-focused on her. Every minute felt like an eternity, each second spent watching her struggle with her pain, her fear. He could see the terror in her eyes as she clutched his hand tightly, the strength of her grip betraying the overwhelming panic she felt.

Ethan's heart ached, knowing there was only so much he could do in this moment. He wished he could take the pain away, erase the fear from her face. His fingers brushed lightly over the back of her hand, offering what little comfort he could. But his mind kept returning to her words—*I don't want to die.* His chest tightened at the thought of losing her, of watching her slip away without being able to do anything to stop it.

Clara's breath came in shallow gasps, and her body trembled as the pain in her head seemed to intensify. The tears that had earlier dried up now flowed freely again,

## Through Tears

unchecked, as she cried softly, her sobs breaking through the silence of the moving ambulance. Her eyes were distant, unfocused, as if she were lost in a fog of confusion and fear.

Her thoughts were chaotic—everything seemed to be spinning out of control. The pain in her head was unlike anything she had ever experienced before, sharp and relentless, as if her very brain were fighting against her. She had no idea what was happening to her, and the uncertainty was more terrifying than the pain itself. Each throb in her skull felt like a cruel reminder that something was horribly wrong.

Clara could barely think through the fog of her fear. *What's happening to me?* She felt trapped in her own body, helpless to stop the storm that was raging inside her. She squeezed Ethan's hand even harder, her fingers trembling, as if his presence was the only thing anchoring her to reality.

Ethan noticed her fear, the way her eyes would flicker with panic, and he leaned closer, his voice low and steady, trying to be the calm in the storm. "Clara, you're going to be okay," he repeated, though he wasn't sure if he believed it himself. But he had to say it—*for her.*

Clara could barely process his words through the haze of her pain and fear. But hearing him speak, seeing the concern in his eyes, gave her a small shred of comfort. She nodded weakly, though her face was still contorted in pain. She didn't want to be this vulnerable, to depend on someone else so completely, but in this moment, she had no choice.

Her thoughts were a whirlwind of anxiety, memories flashing through her mind in a blur—her broken marriage, the years of pain, the loss of control. And now, this—*whatever this was.* She felt small, fragile, as if everything she had worked so hard to rebuild was crumbling before her.

But then, through the panic, there was a quiet part of her that found solace in Ethan's presence. She didn't know how he had become this pillar of strength for her, but she was thankful he was there. In the midst of her darkest fear, she found a small spark of hope—hope that, no matter what happened, she wouldn't face it alone.

The ambulance screeched to a halt at the hospital

# A QUIET ACHE

entrance, and the paramedics quickly sprang into action. Clara was wheeled swiftly through the emergency doors, with Ethan running beside her, his heart pounding in his chest. The lights of the hospital hallways blurred as they moved, the urgency of the situation making everything feel like it was happening in slow motion. The steady beep of the heart monitor filled the air, a stark reminder of the fragility of life.

Clara's face was pale, her eyes barely open as she clung to Ethan's hand. Her breathing was shallow, and every small movement she made seemed to cause her more pain. Ethan's grip tightened around hers, though he could feel his own heart racing. He wished he could take away the agony she was in, but all he could do was be there with her, offering silent support.

As they arrived at the ICU, the medical team was already waiting, prepared to take over. Nurses and doctors moved with practiced efficiency, speaking in low, calm voices as they readied equipment and prepped Clara for immediate treatment. Ethan stepped aside, but he could see the fear in her eyes as she looked up at him, pleading silently for reassurance. He gave her a small, reassuring nod, though his stomach churned with worry.

The doctors quickly began to assess Clara, inserting an IV line and connecting her to various machines that would monitor her vitals. The atmosphere was intense, the room full of a quiet kind of urgency that made Ethan's heart ache. He stood against the wall, his mind racing, trying to make sense of what was happening. But all he could do was watch—watch as Clara was surrounded by a flurry of activity, her pain still evident in the tightness of her face.

The doctor in charge, Nick, turned to Ethan, giving him a brief but professional glance. "We'll need to run some tests immediately," the doctor explained. "It looks like we're dealing with a serious condition, but we need to gather more information. Please wait outside for a moment, and we'll update you as soon as we know more."

Ethan didn't hesitate. He nodded wordlessly, though he wanted nothing more than to stay by Clara's side. But he knew he had to trust the medical team—this was their

# Through Tears

domain now, not his. As they moved Clara into the ICU bed and continued their work, Ethan stepped out of the room, his mind spinning with a thousand thoughts. His heart ached for Clara, and the fear that had gripped him ever since she called him earlier intensified with every passing second.

Outside the ICU, Ethan paced back and forth, his anxiety growing with each minute that passed. *What's happening to her?* The questions swirled in his mind, but there were no answers yet. All he could do was wait—wait for the doctors to tell him what was going on, wait to find out if she would be okay.

Minutes felt like hours. Finally, Dr. Nick returned, his expression serious but not grave. "Clara's condition is serious," the doctor began. "We're still waiting for the test results to confirm, but there are signs of something affecting her brain. It could be a tumor, or something else entirely. We'll need to keep her under observation for now, but we're doing everything we can."

Ethan's breath caught in his throat. *A tumor?* The word echoed in his mind, but he couldn't quite grasp it. He felt numb, his entire body tense with the weight of the uncertainty. He nodded, though the doctor's words didn't fully register.

"Is she going to be okay?" Ethan asked, his voice strained. The doctor hesitated for a moment before replying. "It's too early to say, but we'll know more once the tests come back. For now, all we can do is monitor her closely."

Ethan swallowed hard, trying to steady himself. He couldn't lose Clara—not after everything they had been through. Not after everything she had fought for. But as the doctor left to continue monitoring Clara, Ethan was left standing alone, the uncertainty hanging heavily in the air. He could only pray that Clara would be okay—that somehow, they would both make it through this.

***

Ethan's heart pounded in his chest as time seemed to stretch endlessly. He paced back and forth, his eyes glued to the ICU door, hoping to catch any sign of the doctor. One hour passed, then two, and still no word. Each minute felt like a lifetime, the weight of uncertainty pressing down on

# A QUIET ACHE

him. What if something happens to her? The thought gnawed at him, but he tried to push it away. He couldn't afford to think like that, not now.

Finally, after what felt like an eternity, the door to the ICU opened. Dr. Nick emerged, his face serious, and Ethan's breath caught in his throat as he stood up quickly, his heart racing. The doctor didn't immediately speak, and Ethan's stomach twisted with dread.

"Is she...?" Ethan asked, his voice barely above a whisper.

The doctor took a deep breath and met Ethan's gaze. "Clara has a tumor in her brain," he said quietly, his tone measured but filled with gravity. "We don't have all the details yet—we need to run more tests to determine the type of tumor and the extent of the damage. But it's confirmed that there is a tumor, and it's affecting her brain function."

Ethan felt the floor beneath him shift. The words seemed distant, like they were coming from someone else. A tumor. He couldn't process it at first. The word echoed in his mind, but the shock of it left him momentarily paralyzed. He had never imagined that Clara, the woman he had grown so close to, would be facing something so life-altering.

He clenched his fists, trying to steady his breathing. "Is it... is it treatable?" He asked, his voice trembling with barely contained fear.

The doctor nodded slowly. "There are options, but we need more information. We'll need to run additional imaging and tests to understand the full scope of it. I can't give you a clear answer just yet. But I want to assure you that we're doing everything we can to help her."

Ethan closed his eyes for a brief moment, trying to absorb the information. He didn't know what to feel—there was so much uncertainty. All he could think about was Clara, lying in that sterile room, suffering, and he was helpless to fix it. But one thing was clear: He couldn't leave her now. He couldn't let her face this alone. Couldn't.

"Thank you, doctor" Ethan managed to say, his voice hoarse. "Please, let me know as soon as you have any more information."

Dr. Nick gave him a reassuring nod before walking back

## Through Tears

into the ICU. Ethan stood there, his body heavy with a mix of fear and concern, unable to shake the image of Clara's pain from his mind. He needed to be strong for her, but it felt as though his own strength was faltering.

He sank back down into a chair, his mind racing, his heart aching for her. She had already been through so much. And now, this. The thought of losing her, of her enduring any more pain, was unbearable.

But he knew one thing for sure—he wouldn't leave her side. Not now, not ever. He would be there for her, no matter what happened next.

Ethan sat rigidly, his gaze fixed on the door, his eyes tired but unwavering. Five long hours had passed, the clock's short hand pointing at 8 p.m., and the uncertainty weighed heavily on his chest. The hospital seemed to stretch time itself—each second felt like a decade as his thoughts raced, desperately clinging to any hope that things would be alright for her.

He tried not to let his mind spiral, to focus on the facts, but each passing moment without news made it harder to maintain his composure. *Will she be okay? What's the best way forward?* Questions lingered, unanswered, making the silence in the waiting room even more deafening. He stood when the ICU door finally creaked open, and the doctor stepped out. He rose quickly, his heart hammering in his chest, though his feet felt as though they were cemented to the ground.

The doctor's face was serious but calm, and Ethan's breath caught as he approached.

"Doctor," Ethan said urgently, "How is she? Is she okay?"

The doctor paused before answering, his expression grave. "We've completed the imaging. She has orbital tumors—abnormal tissue growths in the structures surrounding her eye," he said, the words falling like stones into the heavy silence. "These tumors need to be removed. It's a serious situation, but surgery is the next step. We need to move quickly, but with proper care, there's hope."

Ethan felt his stomach drop as the words settled in. *Orbital tumors.* He had known it was bad, but hearing it confirmed made the weight of it all real. The fact that surgery

# A QUIET ACHE

was needed hit him with a cold wave of reality. Yet, despite the urgency, he held onto a thread of hope—the doctor hadn't said it was too late, that there was nothing they could do.

Ethan nodded slowly, trying to absorb the news. "How soon can the surgery be scheduled?" he asked, his voice quieter now, betraying the calm he was trying to maintain.

"We'll need to prepare for surgery within the next 24 hours," the doctor replied. "We're arranging for the necessary tests and making sure she is stable. The sooner we act, the better."

Ethan swallowed, his mind racing. The idea of Clara undergoing surgery, of her being in danger, made his insides twist with fear. But there was no time to waste. He had to be strong for her now, more than ever.

The doctor said, "Now, you can be with her," as he gestured toward the door, signaling for Ethan to enter. "Thank you, doctor," Ethan said, his voice firm but filled with worry. He took a deep breath, trying to steady himself, and walked toward the ICU door. He needed to see her. He needed to be with her.

As Ethan entered the room, his heart ached at the sight of Clara, pale and frail, lying in the bed. But there was something else in her expression, too. A deep vulnerability that he hadn't seen before. And despite the uncertainty ahead, he knew that he would be there, standing beside her, through everything that came next.

Dr. Nick entered the room, his presence a welcome distraction from the heavy silence that had settled over them. He gave Ethan a reassuring glance before turning to Clara. "Ethan stay with you now," he said, his tone warm but professional. "She's stable for the moment, and we've managed the pain."

Ethan's heart skipped a beat. Finally, he could be there, truly there, with her, not as a doctor but as someone who cared deeply for her. Dr. Nick nodded once more, confirming that everything was in place for her recovery. Ethan stepped closer to her bed, looking down at her with a mix of relief and emotion. He brushed a strand of hair from her forehead.

## Through Tears

Clara smiled faintly, her eyes fluttering open to meet his.

"I'm here," Ethan added, his voice filled with tenderness. "I'm not going anywhere, Clara."

Her gaze locked with his, and for a moment, it was as if the world outside the hospital room ceased to exist. They didn't need words; their eyes spoke volumes. And in that silence, the connection between them deepened even further.

Clara's arms wrapped around him, and for a moment, everything else faded away. The fear, the uncertainty, the looming surgery—it all melted into the warmth of this simple embrace. They held each other, not needing to say anything, just feeling the comfort of being together. In that quiet moment, they both found a peace that had eluded them for days.

After a brief silence, she spoke softly, her voice weak and fragile, as if the weight of her emotions were catching up with her. "I'm… fine, Ethan. Don't… worry. I'm also with you."

Ethan closed his eyes, holding her close, grateful for this fleeting moment of calm. Her presence, her quiet strength, was a balm to his soul, and as they hugged, he felt the weight of the world lift, if only for a brief moment. Despite everything that had happened, despite the unknowns ahead, they had each other. And in that moment, they found wholeness.

He sat beside her bed, gently taking her hand as she began to speak. Her voice was still a little shaky, but there was a calmness to it. "I've had this headache… for two years, but it was… never as strong as today," she confessed, looking up at him. "I just thought it was… stress, or pressure… from everything—my mom, the past, life itself. I didn't think it was anything… serious."

Ethan nodded, his gaze softening. He understood all too well how easy it was to dismiss signs when life felt overwhelming. Now he felt it was the right moment to tell her the truth, knowing it was something she had a right to understand. "Clara," he began, his voice steady but filled with care, "I know you never expected it, but the doctors found two tumors in your brain. They need to remove them, but there's a chance that, because of their different locations, you may lose your eyesight."

Clara's tired eyes widened slightly, a flicker of surprise breaking through the weariness etched into her face, but for a little while, she nodded, already processing the weight of his words. Then, she began to sob, her quiet cries breaking through the stillness. Ethan felt a deep, painful stillness within himself, the weight of her sorrow affecting him deeply. "I'm scared, Ethan," she whispered, squeezing his hand. "But I... I don't want to lose my sight. I don't want to live without seeing anything."

Ethan leaned in closer, his voice full of reassurance. "You're not alone in this. Whatever happens, I'll be right here. We'll face it together, every step of the way." He held her gaze, silently promising her that, no matter what, he would be there to help her through the journey ahead.

His heart beat faster as he looked into her eyes, seeing the vulnerability and strength that had always been there, even through her struggles. He knew, deep down, that this was the moment he could no longer keep his feelings hidden.

Taking a deep breath, he leaned in slightly, his voice soft but filled with sincerity. "Clara, I... I love you. More than I ever knew I could. And I want you to see me, to know how much I care about you—about every part of you. I want you to know that, no matter what happens, I'm here. I'm always going to be here. And look at me now, honey. You see me, right?"

Clara's eyes filled with emotion, her hand tightening around his. She couldn't speak right away, but she nodded, feeling the weight of his words settle into her heart. In that moment, she understood the depth of his love—his love for her, for everything she had gone through, and for the strength he saw in her.

She looked at him through her tears, her gaze soft and filled with love, despite the pain she was enduring. "I love you, too, Ethan," she whispered, her voice filled with warmth. "And I'm so happy you're here."

They were with each other in that quiet room, the world outside forgotten, as they shared a quiet, tender moment—one that neither of them would ever forget.

## Through Tears

The air between them seemed to hum with anticipation, the quiet room holding its breath as Ethan gently cupped her face in his hands. His touch was tender, his fingers brushing softly against her skin, feeling the warmth of her presence, so close, so real. Clara's heart raced, her breath shallow, as she looked up at him, her gaze full of vulnerability and trust. The world outside faded away, leaving only the two of them, the connection they had shared all this time now shining in the light of the moment.

Ethan leaned in slowly, his face inches from hers, as if giving her the space to pull away if she needed to. But she didn't pull away. She closed her eyes, her lips slightly parted, and in that silence, everything she had felt for him—every quiet thought, every unsaid word—came rushing to the surface.

And then, finally, their lips met.

At first, it was soft, tentative, as if the world was holding its breath. Neither of them rushed, both feeling the weight of the moment—a moment that had been years in the making. Clara's breath caught in her throat, and Ethan's heart pounded in his chest, the rhythm quickening as though time itself had paused to witness the delicate connection between them.

The kiss deepened, but slowly, as if they were savoring the very act of being in each other's presence after so long apart. Ethan poured every ounce of affection, every bit of care he had ever nurtured for Clara, into that kiss. It was an expression of all the quiet years, the moments of longing, the unspoken promises that had built a foundation for this fragile yet profound act.

Clara responded without hesitation, her hand lifting to rest against his chest, feeling the steady, reassuring beat of his heart. She could feel everything in that kiss—the warmth of his embrace, the gentleness of his touch, and the unwavering support that had always been there, just beneath the surface. And in that fleeting, sacred space between them, she let herself surrender. For so long, she had denied herself the chance to trust the love she had always been too afraid to fully embrace.

## A QUIET ACHE

This kiss wasn't just an expression of passion; it was a culmination of everything they had been through, all the unspoken emotions, all the healing, all the moments of silent understanding. It was a promise—not just of love, but of a future they would now walk into together, hand in hand, hearts fully open.

As they pulled away, their foreheads rested gently against one another, their breaths mingling in the quiet stillness. The weight of the moment seemed to hang in the air, rich with meaning. Neither of them spoke, for there were no words left to say. The kiss had already spoken everything they needed to hear—everything they had felt, everything they hoped for, all bound together in the simple, yet extraordinary act of love.

## CHAPTER SIX

## Physical Eyes that Never Met Again

The tumors were dangerously close to her eyes, and the only option was to remove them—along with her vision. It was a decision that no one should have to make, and he felt helpless in that moment, unable to change the course of her fate.

After the doctors confirmed the surgery, Ethan called his hospital, requesting several days off. It was the least he could do to support Clara during this critical time. He needed to be there for her, to stand by her side as her world shifted, as everything she had known threatened to unravel.

Nothing now is more important than her—Clara.

For the next 24 hours, Ethan remained with Clara, offering her the comfort of his complete presence and strong support. They spoke little, but there was an understanding between them—an unspoken bond that needed no words. They simply sat together, gazing at each other, every minute precious, as if each passing second was a great gift.

Clara, despite the pain and fear, drew strength from Ethan's calm demeanor. Ethan did not judge her for her tears or her fear; instead, he quietly held her hand and reassured her. He let her know, in subtle ways, that she was not alone in this. They were in this together, as they always had been—only now, the stakes were higher, the fears more real.

In the quiet moments, Clara found peace in Ethan's eyes. They were a mirror of everything she had once taken for granted—everything that could soon be lost. And yet, as they looked at each other, there was no pity in Ethan's gaze, only understanding. He saw her, truly saw her, beyond the diagnosis, beyond the fear.

And Clara, in return, gazed into his eyes as if memorizing every detail, every flicker of emotion. She didn't know what the future would hold, but in that moment, with Ethan by her side, she felt a peace she hadn't known in years. No matter what happened, she knew that she would not face it alone. And for the first time in a long while, Clara felt truly seen—by someone who understood her, who loved her not in spite of her struggles, but through them.

The hours passed like this—silent but deeply connected. The weight of the coming surgery, the uncertainty of her future, loomed over them, but they didn't speak of it. Instead, they focused on the present—on their time together, on the moments that felt like precious gems, fragile and fleeting.

Dr. Nick approached Ethan once more, his expression grave and his gesture firm, signaling him to step aside for a private conversation about the final decision. Ethan followed, his heart pounding as he braced for the words he feared. The doctor took a deep breath and spoke with a quiet finality. "We've done everything we could, Ethan. We explored every possible option to save her eyes, but the tumors are too invasive. Removing them is the only way to save her life," the doctor said gently, yet in a firm voice.

Ethan felt the weight of the words sink into his chest like a heavy stone. His hands trembled as he nodded, his mind swirling with emotions—grief, anger, and the overwhelming need to be strong for her.

The hours leading to the surgery felt agonizingly slow, yet unbearably fleeting. Each tick of the clock echoed in Ethan's mind, like the relentless chime of a verdict being delivered.

Tik. Tak. Tik. Tak...

Every second was a reminder of what was coming, of the loss that Clara would have to endure—and one he would carry in his heart.

Ethan sat quietly beside her, his gaze never leaving her. She was so exhausted and had finally drifted into sleep. It was good for her, he thought—she needed to gather her strength for the long hours of surgery ahead.

In her sleep, she looked serene, her beauty even more striking. There was a gentleness to her, a quiet strength born of sacrifice and selflessness. To him, she wasn't just beautiful—she was extraordinary. Then he thought about Clara's eyes—the way they lit up when she laughed, the way

## Physical Eyes That Never Met Again

they softened when she spoke of her mother, and the way they had locked with his in that moment of shared understanding and love. The eyes that could inspire the creation of many beautiful paintings!

Now, he knew, she would never see the world the same way again. She would never see him again. The thought was a blade slicing through his heart. Yet, even through the pain, he resolved to be her strength. He promised himself that he would be her light in the darkness to come.

Hours slipped by like moments to him, each passing second feeling like a thief stealing precious time. He didn't want the clock to move so quickly; it felt merciless, dragging him closer to a reality he wasn't ready to face. The stillness of the room was heavy, and he clung to every fleeting moment of Clara's peaceful sleep, memorizing her face as though it were the last time he'd see her like this.

\*\*\*

Then, breaking the silence, the door creaked open, and Dr. Nick stepped in. Ethan's heart sank at the sight of him. The doctor's calm but firm voice delivered the words Ethan had dreaded: "The surgery is ready now."

Clara's eyes fluttered open, her gaze immediately searching for Ethan. Without hesitation, her first instinct was to reach for his hand, holding it tightly as though anchoring herself to the present. Her grip was gentle but firm, a silent plea for reassurance.

Ethan leaned closer, his face warm with a bittersweet smile. Before he could speak, Clara whispered, "Are you here?"

"I'm here," he replied softly, his voice steady despite the ache in his chest.

Turning to the doctor, Ethan respectfully asked, "Could we have a few minutes alone before... before it begins?"

The doctor nodded with understanding, stepping back and leaving them in the quiet sanctuary of their shared moment. Ethan shifted his chair closer, holding both her

# A QUIET ACHE

hands now, his eyes fixed on hers, knowing that every glance they exchanged was a treasure that would soon become a memory.

Clara's heart raced, but she tried her best to mask the fear swirling inside her. Her trembling hands gripped Ethan's, her knuckles white from the pressure. Yet, in her silence, her eyes did all the speaking. She took in every detail of his face—the strong line of his nose, the softness of his cheeks, the curve of his lips, the subtle strength of his chin. Her gaze lingered on his ears, the hands that had held hers so gently, and finally, his eyes—those deep, kind eyes that had seen her through so much.

She committed it all to memory, engraving him in her heart like an artist painting a masterpiece. Ethan didn't say a word. He simply let her take her time, his steady presence a comfort in her storm of fear. The room seemed to hold its breath for them, quiet and still, as though it, too, understood the weight of this moment.

Then, silently, tears welled up in Clara's beautiful eyes, spilling down her cheeks as she held Ethan's gaze. Her emotions were raw, a mixture of fear, sorrow, and an unspoken gratitude for the man before her. Ethan, though steady on the outside, felt a storm raging within. His tears didn't fall, but they burned deep inside, tightening his chest with a grief he couldn't yet put into words.

He squeezed her hand gently, his thumb brushing over her fingers as if trying to transfer all his strength to her. Neither spoke, but the connection between them said everything. They were holding on to each other, anchoring themselves in this fleeting moment before the storm. It wasn't just sadness—it was love, unyielding and strong, even as time cruelly moved forward.

Then, silently, tears welled up in Clara's beautiful eyes, spilling down her cheeks as she held Ethan's gaze. Her emotions were raw, a mixture of fear, sorrow, and an unspoken gratitude for the man before her. Ethan, though steady on the outside, felt a storm raging within.

He sat there, his heart aching with helplessness. He wished, with every fiber of his being, that he could give her

## Physical Eyes That Never Met Again

one or even both of his eyes. If it meant she could keep seeing the world, he would do it in an instant. But he knew the harsh reality—medicine and technology hadn't reached that point yet.

The thought of her losing the light in her eyes, those eyes that had held so much strength and kindness even through pain, was unbearable. He swallowed hard, forcing himself to stay composed. She needed him strong, not broken. He reached out and gently tucked a strand of hair behind her ear, his touch tender and full of unspoken promises.

Her voice trembled slightly as she spoke, sharing her fears about the unknowns of the surgery and the life ahead without her sight. "I never imagined I'd face something like this," she whispered, her hands clenched tightly in her lap. "It feels like I'm losing everything—my vision, my way of seeing you, seeing the world... and I don't know how to face it."

Ethan's voice was steady but full of emotion. He reached for her hand, gently holding it. "Clara, I'm here. You're not losing me, and you're not losing everything. You're still you, and I'll be with you through it all." She nodded, her eyes searching his face for reassurance. "You're the only one who's made me feel truly seen in years. When I'm with you, I feel understood, cared for. I don't know what the future holds, but I want to keep you close. Always."

Ethan leaned in closer, his forehead touching hers. "I want that too. You've been through more than anyone should, but I believe in you. I believe in us. No matter what happens with your vision, you'll never be alone. I promise."

They stayed in silence for a moment, each feeling the gravity of their words, knowing this might be their last quiet moment together before everything changed. But in that stillness, there was a deep, shared understanding that their bond, however uncertain the future might be, would endure.

"Clara," he whispered softly, "if I could, I'd trade places with you in a heartbeat." His voice cracked just slightly, but his resolve remained firm. All he could do now was be her pillar of support, the one thing he knew she could lean on.

## A QUIET ACHE

She turned her head slightly toward Ethan, her lips trembling as she tried to respond. But no words came. Instead, she reached out, her fingers brushing against his cheek, tracing the contours of his face as if trying to etch them into her memory. Her touch was light, almost hesitant, but it spoke volumes. "I know," she finally whispered, her voice barely audible. "I know you would. And that's enough for me."

She lay still, feeling a heavy weight settle in her chest as she listened to Ethan's words. His promise, his steady reassurance, wrapped around her like a comforting blanket. But the fear that gnawed at her heart couldn't be soothed by words alone. The reality of what was to come—losing her sight, losing the way she had always perceived the world—felt suffocating.

Her mind wandered back to the years before, the life she once had, full of color and clarity. She had taken her vision for granted, never imagining that it would slip away so suddenly. And now, sitting in this sterile hospital room, she realized just how much she had relied on seeing. On seeing Ethan. On seeing the faces of her mother, of the season changes, of the simple beauty in the world around her.

"I'm scared, Ethan," she admitted, her voice barely above a whisper. Her hands trembled, and she instinctively clutched the fabric of her gown. "What if... What if I can't handle it? What if I'm never the same again? What if I can't... I can't see you anymore?" Her words faltered, and a sob caught in her throat.

Ethan squeezed her hand, his gaze unwavering, as if he could anchor her with his presence alone. "You'll still have me. Even if you can't see me, I'll always be here with you. I won't leave you. Not now, not ever."

But Clara, lost in her own thoughts, couldn't help but imagine a future where her world was shrouded in darkness. She had always been so independent, so strong, but now she felt like she was being asked to surrender a part of herself that was essential. Her identity. Her connection to the world.

"I've always been able to see," she murmured, tears slipping down her cheeks. "Now, I'm not sure who I'll be without it. Without my eyes, without seeing everything that makes life... life. How do I even begin to live in a world that's just... dark... forever?"

His heart ached as he watched her wrestle with the fear that consumed her. He wished he could take her pain away, give her the answers she so desperately sought. But all he could do was promise to walk with her through the unknown, to be her strength when she felt too weak to carry on.

"You'll find your way," he said softly, his voice steady. "You're stronger than you know. And I'll be right there with you, helping you see the world in a way you never imagined. You'll discover new ways of experiencing life, ways that don't depend on what you can see, but on what you feel, what you hear, what you experience."

She closed her eyes for a moment, the warmth of his words sinking in, but the fear still loomed large. She didn't know how to let go of her past life. She didn't know how to move forward without the certainty of her vision. But in that moment, with Ethan's hand in hers, she realized that, maybe, just maybe, she didn't have to walk this path alone.

Ethan held her hand against his face, closing his eyes for a moment, letting himself feel the weight of her emotions. He didn't care if the world saw his strength falter; for Clara, he'd bare every ounce of vulnerability if it meant giving her the comfort she needed.

The room was quiet except for the faint hum of the machines monitoring Clara's vitals. Every tick of the clock seemed louder, heavier, as if counting down the moments they had left before the surgery.

"I'll be here," Ethan said firmly, his eyes locking onto hers. "Every step of the way."

Clara nodded, her tears still flowing silently. "Thank you," she whispered. "For everything... For being here when I didn't even know I needed someone."

Ethan leaned closer, his forehead lightly touching hers. "You don't have to thank me," he said softly. "This is where I want to be. With you."

# A QUIET ACHE

As Ethan sat quietly, embracing her on her hospital bed, his gaze fixed on her anxious and fragile face, his heart felt heavier than it ever had. The thought of Clara's eyes—the very eyes that had once sparkled with light and looked at him with warmth and understanding—about to be taken away filled him with a sorrow he could hardly bear.

Those eyes weren't just hers; they were windows to her soul, reflections of her hidden strength, and reminders of the unspoken moments they had shared.

Ethan's mind raced with memories: the way her eyes sparkled with joy when she laughed with high school friends, the excitement in them as she talked about her dreams, the tears they held when she opened up about her struggles with family and her marriage, and the gentle gaze that made him feel a happiness no one else ever had. He couldn't imagine a world where those eyes, so full of life and meaning, would no longer meet his in the same way.

He kept gazing into Clara's eyes, and he could tell that they were windows to a soul that seemed both fragile and strong at once, like a delicate porcelain vase that had weathered years of storms yet remained intact. In their depths, he could sense the weight of countless unspoken stories, of battles fought silently and endured in solitude. There was a vulnerability in them, a soft flicker of sorrow, as if they had witnessed too much of life's harshness, yet they never lost their quiet resilience. Her gaze, steady yet gentle, reflected a strength forged through pain, a deep-rooted endurance that seemed unshakable despite the fragility that surrounded it. Those eyes, full of grace and wisdom, hinted at a spirit that had been tested but had never broken, quietly powerful in a way that left anyone who looked into them both awestruck and humbled.

Yet, amidst the anguish, he found himself clinging to a glimmer of hope. Clara's eyes might soon be gone, but her essence—the love, courage, and resilience she carried—was something no surgery could ever take away. It was in her words, her touch, and her presence. Ethan knew that while her vision would change, the way he saw her would never waver. In his heart, she was still the woman whose beauty and strength radiated far beyond her eyes.

As he sat there, his hands clenched tightly in his lap, Ethan silently vowed to be her strength when she felt weak, her light when the darkness closed in. No matter what lay ahead, he would be there—offering her the comfort of his unwavering love and the promise that she would never face this alone.

Ethan's thoughts spiraled further, each one tugging at his heart. He couldn't stop thinking about how much she had endured—the battles she fought silently, the sacrifices she made for others, and now this. It felt cruel, unjust, that someone so kind and full of grace would have to endure yet another loss. He wanted to scream at the universe, to demand why it was her, why it had to take something so precious from her. But he swallowed those feelings, knowing Clara didn't need his anger; she needed his presence, his love.

As he glanced at her resting form, the soft rise and fall of her chest, he tried to imagine what she might be feeling. How could someone prepare for such a big loss? Did she feel fear? Was she angry? Or was she simply resigned to it, too tired to fight against the tide anymore? He wished he could trade places with her, take on her pain, her fears, her burdens. But all he could do was be here, holding onto her with every fiber of his being, silently willing her to feel his strength.

He thought about her life after the surgery—how she might struggle to adjust, how the world she had always seen would now be a patchwork of memories and sensations. Ethan resolved that he would not let her feel alone in this. He would be her guide if she needed it, her constant in a world that might feel unfamiliar and frightening. He would describe sunsets for her, paint her the vivid landscapes she once loved to gaze upon, and remind her every day of the beauty she carried within her, a beauty that no surgery could ever erase.

But more than anything, Ethan realized that this was his moment to prove his love—to show her that his feelings for her weren't just born from admiration or affection, but from a deep, unshakable bond. Her loss was his loss; her pain, his pain; her happiness, his happiness. And in her journey ahead, he would not falter. He would be her anchor, her calm in the storm, the person she could always lean on, even in the darkest moments.

***

The nurse gently knocked on the door, signaling that it was time. Ethan pulled back slightly, his hands still holding hers, reluctant to let go.

"You'll be okay," he said, his voice steady, though his heart felt broken. "Honey! I'll be right here when you wake up."

Clara nodded again, her grip tightening for a moment before she let go, as the nurse wheeled her bed down the corridor toward the operating room.

Clara, in the final seconds, tried to look at Ethan with her own eyes, as if she wanted to capture the image of him in her memory, like a photograph, to keep him forever in her mind. Ethan stood frozen, his eyes following her until the doors closed behind her.

He leaned back against the wall, his hands covering his face as the weight of the moment finally settled in. He felt helpless, but he knew he had to stay strong—for her. The weight of it pressed down on him like a thousand stones. As tears stung his eyes, he whispered softly, to himself, "I will still see you, Clara. I will always see you."

The words were a promise, a vow that his love for her would transcend what the eyes could see. He would hold her in his heart, in his soul, and in every quiet moment they shared, even if she couldn't see him. His love would be her vision when the world went dark. He would be her light, and nothing, not even this, could take that away.

## CHAPTER SEVEN
# The Third Eye

After eight and a half long hours, the double doors of the operating room finally opened, and the nurse emerged, gently pushing Clara on a gurney. Her head was wrapped in white bandages, covering the place where her beautiful eyes had once sparkled with life. She was still under the effects of the anesthesia, her body looked pale. The nurse wheeled her into the special care unit, leaving Ethan behind the closed doors once more.

Ethan sat motionless in the hallway, his eyes fixed on the doors, willing the doctor to appear with an update. Time had stretched endlessly, but his hope refused to waver. Dr. Nick approached, his face a blend of exhaustion and compassion. "The surgery went as planned," he said, his voice steady but soft. "She's stable now, but it will take time for her to recover—physically and emotionally."

Ethan nodded, swallowing hard against the lump in his throat. "Thank you, doctor," he murmured. His gratitude was genuine, but his heart ached at the reality they now faced. He was ushered into the room where Clara lay, and the sight of her so still, so fragile, nearly broke him. The chair by her bedside became his anchor as he sat down, taking her hand gently in his.

Hours passed, and finally, Clara stirred. Her fingers twitched in his, and a soft moan escaped her lips. Holding her hand tightly, Ethan leaned closer, his voice tender. "Sweetheart, I'm here."

Her lips parted, and she whispered, "Ethan?" Her voice was weak, but it carried the familiar warmth that he cherished. She reached up instinctively but hesitated, her hand hovering near her face as if afraid to confirm what she already knew. Tears pooled in Ethan's eyes as he guided her hand back down, holding it tightly.

"It's okay," he said softly. "I'm right here. You're not alone."

Clara turned her head slightly toward his voice, her

# A QUIET ACHE

expression a mix of vulnerability and courage. "I... can't see, Ethan," she whispered, her voice trembling. "All... gone."

Ethan's heart shattered at her words. He didn't know what to say now, but he steadied himself, knowing she needed his strength. "Clara, you may not see with your eyes anymore, but you'll see with something much deeper—your heart, your soul. That's the kind of sight that can never be taken away."

Clara's lips quivered, and silent tears traced paths down her cheeks. "I'm... scared. Dark...!" she admitted, her voice barely audible.

"I know," Ethan whispered, brushing her tears away with the back of his hand. "But you're not alone in this. I'm here, sweetheart. Every step of the way, I'll be with you."

They sat in silence for a moment, the gravity of the situation settling around them like a heavy fog. Then, Clara's trembling hand reached out, searching for him. Ethan guided her fingers to his face, letting her explore the contours of his nose, his cheeks, his lips.

"I... want to remember you like this," she said softly. "Even if I can't see you, I'll always... know you."

Ethan couldn't hold back the tears any longer. They slipped down his face as he held her hand against his cheek. "And I'll always see you, sweetheart," he said, his voice thick with emotion. "Not just with my eyes, but with my heart. You're more beautiful than ever."

\*\*\*

Dr. Nick checked on her every morning with a reassuring presence. The nurses diligently took turns changing her bandages, handling her with care and compassion. The wounds on her head were healing steadily, but her face had changed profoundly. The empty spaces where her eyes had stayed were now covered with healing skin, a stark reminder of what had been lost. Day by day, the physical wounds mended, but the emotional weight lingered, heavy and unspoken.

Sometimes, during the stillness of certain nights, Ethan would quietly watch her as she sobbed softly, trying to hide her pain. He understood her sorrow, though not completely—he hadn't lived through her exact experience. Yet, he could imagine the depth of her fear and grief. To live in a world without the light of day, without the soft glow of the moon at night, seemed unimaginably dark. For her, every hour now felt like an endless night, a darkness both outside and within. His heart ached, knowing he could only share her burden, but never truly take it away.

Ethan could sense the quiet despair that Clara tried so hard to conceal, though her attempts were futile in his eyes. There was something hopeless in her heart now, something that settled deeply within her, like a shadow that no amount of light could chase away. He watched her, knowing that she was doing her best to mask it, to hold onto some semblance of strength, but beneath her composed exterior, her mind was consumed with an overwhelming sense of loss.

"What time is it now, Ethan?" She asked softly, her voice trembling as she tried to suppress the deep sadness inside her. It wasn't that she really needed to know the time—it was the longing to connect with the world she could no longer see. Somewhere deep down, she wanted to imagine the sky—was it bright or dull? Was the sun shining warmly or hiding behind gloomy clouds?

His heart sank as he looked at her, sensing the ache in her unspoken thoughts. Swallowing his own sorrow, he replied gently, "It's 2 p.m. now, honey." He wished he could paint the sky for her with his words, let her feel the light through him. But all he could do was hold her hand a little tighter, silently vowing to be her connection to the world she could no longer see.

Ethan knew that the surgery would remove the tissues around her eyes, along with two optic nerves and the cranial nerves responsible for sight. As a result, she was cast into complete darkness, unable to perceive even the faintest light. The only sensation that remained was the warmth of the sun on her cheeks and forehead. She had entered a new world, one shaped by touch, sensation, and intuition.

Clara's appearance had changed drastically, a stark reminder of the trials she had endured. Her once vibrant and expressive eyes were now hidden beneath layers of bandages,

# A QUIET ACHE

wrapped around her shaved head, the result of the brain surgery. The transformation had turned her into a different woman—a woman shaped by both resilience and profound loss.

Her body had grown thinner, her cheeks hollow, and her skin paler than before. The energy she once radiated seemed dimmed, replaced by a quiet strength and vulnerability. She sat with a stillness that he hadn't seen before, as though every movement now required more thought, more effort.

But even in this fragile state, there was something profound in her presence—a quiet dignity, a depth of spirit that had grown in the absence of physical sight. It was as if, though her outer appearance had altered, her soul had grown louder, shining through in her soft words, her careful gestures, and the quiet courage she exuded with every breath. To Ethan, she was still beautiful, though in a way that now felt transcendent, beyond the surface.

Clara's voice trembled as she asked, "Ethan, how is Mom? Is she okay?" Her hands gripped the edge of the blanket, as if bracing herself for the answer, and she whispered softly to herself, 'I'm sorry, Mom. I can't help you the way I used to.'

Ethan leaned closer, his voice calm and steady, though his heart ached for her. "Don't worry. I check on her every day. She's doing fine, honey." He paused, offering a reassuring smile she couldn't see but could feel in his tone. "I've arranged for a kind woman to care for her around the clock. She's in good hands."

She let out a small, relieved sigh, her lips curving into a faint smile. "Thank you, Ethan… for everything."

He reached out and gently took her hand, his thumb brushing over her knuckles. "You don't have to thank me. This is what family does." His words were simple but filled with meaning, carrying the weight of his unwavering support.

The days that followed were a testament to Clara's resilience and Ethan's unwavering devotion. Though she mourned the loss of her sight, she began to discover a new way of perceiving the world. He became her guide, both within the hospital walls and beyond, helping her navigate the physical struggles and the emotional weight she carried. Together, they discovered beauty in life's simplest moments—the gentle warmth of the sun on her face, the soothing melody of birdsong drifting through the hospital window, and the comforting sensation of soft grass beneath her feet.

***

As she drifted into a peaceful sleep, Ethan quietly slipped out of the room, careful not to disturb her. His heart heavy with concern, he made his way back to Clara's mother's home. He knew she needed him, even if she couldn't always express it. The delicate balance of caring for both of them weighed on him, but he understood that it was in these moments of quiet responsibility that love was most deeply shown—through small acts, without the need for recognition.

In love, everything becomes more bearable.

When Ethan arrived at Clara's mother's home, he was met with a soft, quiet sobbing. Clara's mother sat in her favorite chair, her face streaked with tears that seemed to flow without reason, as though she couldn't fully grasp the pain she felt. A woman, hired to care for her during Clara's hospital stay, was nearby, looking unsure of what to do. He immediately knelt beside her mother, gently taking her hand in his. He spoke softly to her, offering comforting words even though he knew she might not fully understand them. With a calm presence, he helped her settle back into her chair, wiping away her tears and offering a tender smile, reminding her that she was not alone. Though she couldn't remember the details, he understood that what mattered most in that moment was simply being there—offering the love and reassurance she needed.

He knew that Clara's mother's instincts were still sharp in some ways, despite the fog of dementia clouding her mind. She sensed that something was wrong, that there was a shift in the air, a subtle unease—but she couldn't grasp exactly what it was.

Her mother's eyes, full of confusion and sadness, searched his face as if looking for answers, but the words she needed to understand eluded her. Yet, in that moment, he

## A QUIET ACHE

recognized that her love, her protective instinct as a mother, still lingered deep within her, even if she couldn't fully comprehend it. He gently reassured her, offering her the comfort she needed without needing to explain everything. He could feel her unspoken worry, and he knew, even in her fractured state, that she was still very much Clara's mother.

Through the eye of his heart, he saw Clara's mother in a light that transcended her fading memories. To him, she was not just the woman whose mind was slipping away, but a mother who had given everything for her daughter, a woman who still carried the echoes of a lifetime of love and sacrifice. The years of hard work, the struggles, the joy of raising Clara—he could see all of it, not in the words she could no longer remember, but in the quiet, tender moments she shared with her daughter. It was as if her heart, the core of who she was, still communicated in ways that memory could not touch.

Ethan felt a deep reverence for her mother, not out of pity, but out of admiration for the strength of a love that had endured the ravages of time and illness. He understood that while her memories may fade, the essence of who she was—the love, the care, the unspoken connection she had with Clara—remained as vibrant as ever. In her quiet moments, when she reached for Clara's hand or smiled without words, he saw the heart of a mother, as present and strong as it had ever been.

Ethan, too, began to realize something deeper about himself. He saw now that his own love for Clara had been influenced by the love he had witnessed in others, including Clara's mother. It was the love that didn't require perfection, that didn't rely on memory or recognition to exist. It was the love that simply was, in its purest and most enduring form, and he realized that this was the kind of love he could offer—love without expectation, love without time limits, love that simply accepted and embraced the other for who they were, in that moment.

As he observed Clara's mother, Ethan silently thanked her—for giving Clara life, for showing him what real love looked like, even in its most fragile state. Her love, despite the fading of her mind, would always be a part of Clara, and a part of him. And that thought gave him a quiet sense of peace, knowing that some things—like love—were impervious to time and change.

He learned more than he ever expected from the imperfections of Clara and her mother. In Clara, he saw a woman who had been through immense struggles, whose sight had faded but whose inner vision had grown stronger. She was not perfect—no one was—but her resilience, her ability to love and to be loved despite her brokenness, was what truly captivated him. Clara's imperfections made her real, made her human, and it was through those flaws that he saw the raw beauty of her spirit. Her journey wasn't about overcoming every obstacle flawlessly; it was about embracing the imperfections with grace and courage. And in that, he found not only admiration but also a deep understanding of the fragility and strength of the human heart.

Clara's mother, too, taught him valuable lessons in imperfection. Her mind was slipping away, leaving behind fragments of who she once was, but Ethan could see how her love remained steady, even in her confusion. He learned that imperfection did not negate the power of love—it deepened it. Clara's mother, despite her dementia, still reached for her daughter, still shared moments of tenderness and care. It wasn't about remembering every detail or keeping up with every conversation; it was about the feeling, the connection, the heart-to-heart moments that remained untouched by time. Her imperfections only highlighted the depth of her humanity, and he began to understand that love wasn't about being flawless, but about being present—about showing up for each other, even when you couldn't remember the past or predict the future.

Ethan began to see that life itself was a collection of imperfections. The struggles, the flaws, the mistakes—these were not things to be ashamed of, but part of what made the human experience so rich. In loving Clara, and in witnessing her mother's struggle, he learned that it wasn't the absence of imperfection that mattered, but the presence of love in the face of it. To love someone was to accept their imperfections,

## A QUIET ACHE

to cherish them even more because of them, and to find strength in the ways those imperfections shaped their story.

Through her and her mother, Ethan realized that the real beauty of life lay not in perfection, but in embracing each other's humanity. His love for Clara had deepened in ways he hadn't expected. It was no longer about the idealized version of love he had once dreamed of, but about the love that had grown in the soil of their shared struggles. And in this love, he found something far greater than he had ever imagined: a love that was unconditional, unmeasurable, and real—one that bore all things, believed all things, and endured through every imperfection.

Ethan's thoughts drifted deeper as he observed her mother, her condition serving as a poignant reminder of the fragile nature of the human mind. With his background, he understood the complexities of dementia—the way it slowly stripped away the past, blurring the lines between memories and reality. Yet, what struck him most was the power of love, which seemed to transcend the fading of her memory. He saw how her mother still reached for her daughter, as if in the quiet certainty that love was the one thing that could never be lost, even when the mind itself began to unravel.

This realization filled him with a new sense of understanding. He had spent so much of his life trying to make sense of the world through knowledge and reason, but now he saw that the most profound truths were often those that could not be explained, only felt. He thought about his own life and the love that had shaped him—his parents, Clara, and the relationships he had built over the years. The love they shared was not perfect, but it was real, and that was enough. It was the love that had guided him, comforted him, and given him the strength to face his own struggles.

***

Coming back to the hospital, that quiet evening, Ethan stepped into Clara's room. She was awake now, her face turned toward the faint light filtering through the curtains. Hearing his footsteps, she turned her head slightly.

"You're here," Clara said softly, her voice tinged with surprise and relief.

# The Third Eye

"Of course, sweetheart" Ethan replied, a gentle smile crossing his face.

He reached for her hand, wrapping it in his own. "Come with me," he said, his voice tender. "There's something I want to show you."

Without hesitation, she let him help her up. Ethan guided her carefully, his arm steadying her as they made their way to the hospital's serene garden. The soft glow of the setting sun painted the world in warm hues, and the gentle rustling of leaves set a calming rhythm in the air. They reached a bench tucked beneath a canopy of trees, and he helped her sit down.

"This feels peaceful," she murmured, tilting her face toward the breeze. "Tell me... what does it look like?"

Ethan's thumb brushed lightly over her fingers as he began to describe the scene. "The sun is low, casting everything in gold. The flowers are blooming—roses, lilacs, and a few daisies, scattered like they're dancing in the breeze. The trees are swaying, and the sky is a mix of amber and soft lavender. It's... alive, but gentle."

She smiled faintly, her head tilting slightly toward him. "Thank you," she whispered. "For seeing it for me."

They sat in comfortable silence for a while, hand in hand, the stillness around them alive with unspoken words. Ethan finally broke the silence, his voice soft.

"Clara, I don't need my eyes to see what matters most. Being here with you, this... this is all I've ever wanted."

Her grip on his hand tightened slightly. "I don't always know how to be strong."

"You don't have to be," he said, turning toward her. "We'll be strong together."

The words hung between them, as steady and grounding as the earth beneath their feet. Though neither spoke further, the moment was full—a quiet testament to the connection they shared, forged through love, loss, and an unyielding belief in one another.

Clara spoke, her voice steady and filled with a quiet strength. "You were right, honey. There's more to seeing than just using your eyes. I'm learning to see with my heart now, and it's showing me things I never noticed before."

## A QUIET ACHE

He smiled, his heart swelling with pride and love. "The third eye," he said softly. "The one that sees beyond what's visible. You've always had it, sweetheart. You just needed to trust it." His voice softened, carrying a depth of emotion that seemed to fill the room. "Sweetheart," he began, "we all have an invisible eye, one that can see through things we don't fully understand. It's the eye of the soul, the heart. We don't always know how to use it or nourish it, but it's there. And it's so powerful."

Clara tilted her head slightly, listening intently.

"The invisible world," he continued, "is so much more precious and valuable than the visible one. It's where love, hope, and faith reside. It's where true connection is born. And Clara..." He paused, his grip on her hand tightening just slightly. "I know you have this eye. I've known it since the first time I saw you again, sitting on that bench downtown. There was something in you—something deeper than what anyone could see with their physical eyes. It's like your soul reaches out to others, even when you're hurting."

Clara's lips trembled, and she took a shaky breath. "But... how can I learn to rely on this... this invisible eye? I'm so scared of living in darkness."

Ethan leaned closer, his forehead almost touching hers. "You won't be in darkness. You'll see with your heart, with your spirit. And I'll be here every step of the way to remind you that light isn't just something that comes from the sun. It's something that glows from within. And sweetheart,... you shine brighter than you realize."

Tears slipped down her cheeks as she nodded, his words filling the void left by her fear. "Thank you, Ethan," she whispered. "I don't know what I'd do without you."

"You'll never have to find out," he said softly, brushing away her tears.

He sat silently beside her, his mind swirling with admiration and an ache he couldn't quite put into words. He had learned in medical school about the stages of grief—how people often react with denial, anger, or explosive frustration when faced with life-altering changes. It was human nature to resist the unbearable, to lash out when reality felt too harsh to accept.

But Clara... Clara had shown something different. Since the surgery, she hadn't burst into anger or bitter disappointment. Instead, she grew quieter, her voice softer, her presence calm, even in the midst of her pain. He marveled at her strength. It wasn't a loud or dramatic kind of resilience—it was the quiet, unyielding courage of someone choosing to move forward despite the immense weight pressing down on them.

He thought about how easy it would've been for her to crumble under the enormity of what had happened. To scream at the unfairness of it all. And yet, she didn't. She chose grace. Her response wasn't just a testament to her character—it was something deeper, something profound.

Looking at her now, resting after so many difficult days, he felt his admiration for her deepen into something even more profound. She wasn't just surviving—she was teaching him what it meant to endure with dignity and courage.

He leaned back in his chair, his gaze never leaving her. "My sweetest," he whispered under his breath, too softly for her to hear, "you are the strongest person I've ever met. And I love you more with every moment."

Clara turned her face toward him, her sightless eyes filled with a light that no physical vision could match. "I love you too, and I do see you, honey," she said, her voice filled with a quiet certainty. "I see you in a way I never did before. Thank you for being my eyes, my strength, my everything."

Ethan took her hand in his, their fingers intertwining. "And thank you, Clara, for showing me what it means to truly see."

Ethan leaned closer, his hand gently brushing Clara's cheek, careful not to disturb the bandages that wrapped around her head. Her face, though changed, radiated a quiet beauty, one born of strength and acceptance. She turned toward him, her lips trembling as if searching for the right words but finding none.

Their hearts spoke what words could not. Slowly, their lips met in a kiss that carried the weight of everything unspoken—love, pain, hope, and a promise to face the unknown together. It wasn't hurried or fleeting but profound, a meeting of two souls who understood each other in ways that transcended the physical world.

In that moment, time seemed to pause. The room, the hardships, and the uncertainty faded away, leaving only the quiet harmony of two hearts beating as one, both of them breathing deeply, as if drawing strength from one another.

Ethan whispered, "We'll get through this, sweetheart. Together."

She smiled faintly, her fingers finding his. "I know," she replied softly. "I feel it. With you, I feel it."

And in that quiet hospital room, amid the struggles they had endured and the challenges still ahead, their love became a beacon—an unshakable bond that would guide them through the darkness.

In that moment, under the fading light of the evening sky, they discovered a love that transcended the physical, a bond rooted in the deepest parts of their souls. Though Clara's eyes could no longer see, her third eye—the eye of her heart—had opened wide, revealing a world more vivid and beautiful than she had ever known.

***

It was a quiet Saturday afternoon, the kind that seemed to stretch lazily under the weight of the sun. Clara sat in the front yard of Ethan's house, her hands resting softly in her lap, a gentle breeze stirring the hair around her face.

Two weeks had passed since she was discharged from the hospital, and while her body had begun to heal, the emotional ache—deep and persistent—lingered. The silence between the earth and sky mirrored her quiet, introspective mood.

Ethan had just returned from a long shift at the hospital, his scrubs slightly crumpled from hours of constant motion. His tired eyes softened as he approached the front yard, drawn first to Clara, then to the quiet figure of her mother seated on the porch. Clara's mother, a fragile presence in the light of the afternoon, had insisted on staying with Ethan ever since Clara's discharge. The struggle with dementia was visible, though not constant—some days, she recognized her daughter with a warmth that mirrored the past, while other

# The Third Eye

days, the confusion overcame her.

Today was one of those days.

As Clara's mother looked at her, her gaze momentarily turned cold. She didn't recognize Clara because her head was shaved, and she was wearing black glasses. "Who are you?" suddenly the mother said, her voice trembling with fear, "Her face... beautiful, yours isn't." Her words hung in the air, sharp and painful. Clara's heart tightened at the cruelty of the disease, but she didn't flinch. Instead, she offered her mother a gentle smile, her quiet patience filling the space between them. She had learned not to take the words personally, to offer kindness even when it was hard, even when her heart broke in places no one could see.

Ethan stood a few steps away, his gaze lingering on Clara's mother. The words struck him too, deep in his chest, but he knew better than to speak. Instead, he sat next to Clara, the unspoken pain between them shared in the silence. He was there to support, but in moments like this, all he could offer was his presence. Clara's mother didn't always remember her daughter, but Clara, with all her grace, never stopped showing up. The quiet strength she carried through each moment—her enduring love, even in the face of such cruelty from the disease—was something Ethan marveled at, and it filled him with a sorrowful respect.

The afternoon continued in soft quiet, each person lost in their own thoughts, the ebb and flow of Clara's mother's emotions the only movement in the stillness.

Then Ethan felt a quiet warmth fill his chest as he stood on the porch, looking at Clara and her mother. There was something deeply fulfilling about having them here, in his humble house, radiated a quiet charm, a sanctuary carved from simplicity and lived-in warmth. It wasn't just the walls and furniture that made it special—it was the life he had carefully cultivated around him.

The front yard, where Clara sat, was an explosion of color and life. Ethan had carefully planted various flowers, each one chosen not only for its beauty but for the calm it would bring to his heart and to her mother as she sat there watching. The bright orange marigolds seemed to dance in the wind, their warm hue offering a sense of cheerfulness, while the lavender, with its soothing scent, provided a gentle calmness that wrapped around the yard like a soft blanket. There were also soft daisies, their delicate white petals standing in quiet contrast to the bold colors surrounding them, creating a sense of balance and peace. The flowers, with their steady bloom, were like small moments of joy in an otherwise unpredictable world.

The garden was more than just a collection of plants; it was a sanctuary for the senses. The flutter of butterflies drifting lazily between blossoms, the hum of bees gathering nectar, and the gentle sway of the grasses in the breeze all worked together to create an atmosphere of serenity. It was a place where Clara's mother, often lost in the confusing twists of her mind, could find moments of stillness. The simple beauty of nature, ever constant in its cycles, could offer her a kind of solace that no words could.

Ethan had noticed how her mother, even in her more confused moments, would settle into the rhythm of the yard. Sometimes she would sit for hours peacefully, her gaze fixed on the flowers, her brow furrowed in thought, but there was a softness in her eyes when she looked at the blooms. The world outside her mind, the steady pulse of nature, seemed to anchor her, even if only for a fleeting moment. The colors, the movement, and the gentle sounds of the garden spoke to her in ways that were beyond logic. In those moments, the anxiety that sometimes clouded her face would soften, if only briefly, and the peace that filled the air would settle around her like a gentle touch.

It was a subtle kind of healing—one that didn't demand anything, one that simply existed, quietly and beautifully. Ethan smiled to himself as he observed the tranquility the garden provided, knowing that it was doing its quiet work, offering peace in ways words never could.

He took great care in tending to his garden, as if each flower was a prayer, a symbol of peace he wanted to share with the world. The hum of bees moving from bloom to bloom, the flutter of butterflies that danced through the air—these were the sounds of his days, as much a part of the

*The Third Eye*

house as the wooden floors beneath his feet.

In addition to the garden, there were the canaries. Seven cages hung in various spots around the yard, their little golden bodies a delicate contrast against the vibrant backdrop of flowers. Their soft songs filled the air, the sweet, sacred sound a balm to the soul. Ethan had always believed in the power of birdsong to heal—to remind us of the beauty of life, even in its most challenging moments. The canaries weren't just pets; they were a living, breathing prayer, their songs offering peace and comfort to anyone who needed it.

He had carefully chosen each canary, knowing that their melodies would bring light into the house. Clara, with her love for art, would surely appreciate their presence. She had always found solace in the natural rhythms of sound, the music of the world around her. And the birds, with their soft, lilting songs, were the perfect companions for her—quiet, tender, and full of grace. He believed the sound of the canaries, mingled with the rustling of the leaves in the trees, was the greatest comfort Clara could have, a form of healing more powerful than any words could offer.

The trees in the yard, tall and wise, whispered their own symphony as the wind moved through them. Their branches swayed gently, creating a soft, constant murmur—like the earth itself was singing. Ethan often found himself sitting there, surrounded by the natural music of his small sanctuary, feeling a sense of peace wash over him. It wasn't just a refuge for Clara and her mother; it was a place where Ethan, too, could heal.

Every being is broken, he thought, as he sat quietly on the porch, the weight of the thought settling deeply within him. It wasn't a thought born out of bitterness, but out of a kind of acceptance—an understanding that the fractures we carry aren't always visible, but they shape us just the same.

And then he thought of Clara. She, too, carried her own kind of brokenness. The scars of the hospital, the pain of healing, the weight of caregiving—it was all a kind of fracture. But she had learned to embrace it, to live with it, even to find strength in it. She was the quiet testament to the beauty that could emerge from brokenness—a beauty that didn't shy

# A QUIET ACHE

away from the cracks, but rather danced around them, letting the light shine through in unexpected ways.

Ethan's own brokenness was more subtle, perhaps, than most—more like a quiet ache that settled into the bones over time, made evident in moments of exhaustion or loneliness. It wasn't something he would speak of to anyone, not even Clara. But as he observed the garden, the birds, the trees that swayed gently in the breeze, he felt a kind of peace in knowing that brokenness didn't have to be something to hide. It could be something to embrace, to nurture, as the earth nurtured the flowers that bloomed despite the harshest of seasons.

As he walked back to join Clara, he couldn't help but think that this, this humble home with its vibrant plants and healing sounds, was exactly what they all needed. The beauty of it wasn't in its size or grandeur, but in its simplicity—the way the flowers bloomed, the canaries sang, and the trees whispered their wisdom. Here, amidst nature's embrace, healing could happen, not in grand gestures, but in the quiet moments, the soft songs, and the stillness of time spent together.

He had never envisioned his life becoming a sanctuary for someone else, but there was something about her quiet strength and her mother's fragile condition that made him want to offer more—something that felt deeper than simple hospitality.

His home wasn't large or grand, far from the spacious and well-kept house Clara's parents had once lived in. There were no luxurious amenities, no polished floors or ornate furniture. The walls were lined with books and simple photographs, reflecting a life lived in service to others. His kitchen was small, the counter often cluttered with the remnants of his hasty meals between shifts, but it was full of the warmth of a person who lived for comfort, not perfection. It was a space where the smell of fresh herbs from his small garden lingered, and the faint hum of a quiet radio often provided background to his solitude.

But despite the modesty of his surroundings, Ethan knew that peace thrived here. It wasn't a house built for grandeur, but for empathy. Every corner of the space seemed to cradle the quiet moments—moments where Clara could sit without the constant hum of expectations, where her mother could rest in safety, even if the confusion of dementia came and went. He had no illusions about the challenges ahead; he knew the care and attention required to help Clara's mother would demand much of him. But he also knew that in this house, there was something that would heal them both—something that Clara had already sensed when she had accepted his offer.

As he walked back into the house, the familiar sense of peace wrapped around him, the walls of his little home offering a kind of sanctuary he hadn't realized he needed. He glanced at the couch where her mother now sat, her frail hands resting in her lap, her gaze distant one moment and sharp the next. And then there was Clara, her presence, a quiet, steady force in the room. She didn't need to say much; her grace and gentleness were enough.

Ethan smiled to himself as he sat beside her. There was a fullness in his heart that came from offering this space to them—a sense that he wasn't just caring for two people who were suffering, but that he was also being gifted something in return. The humility of the house didn't diminish the love within it. Here, in this modest home, was a refuge not just for the body, but for the soul. And for that, he felt deeply grateful.

"This place is yours, too," Ethan said quietly, more to himself than to Clara, though she caught his words and gave him a small, knowing smile. It was simple, and it wasn't perfect, but for the first time in a long while, it felt like exactly what they all needed.

***

Ethan's approach to caring for her mother was a blend of gentle patience and quiet humor, woven with moments of tenderness that brought lightness to even the most difficult days. His home had become a haven for them—a place where healing wasn't forced, but quietly unfolded, even amidst the challenges of blindness and dementia.

One afternoon, as the sun dipped lower in the sky, Clara's

mother sat outside on the porch, her fragile hands resting on a crochet blanket spread across her lap. Though her memory often betrayed her, she seemed calm in the moment, her gaze drawn to the colors of the garden that he had so carefully nurtured. He had just finished feeding the canaries, their soft, melodious songs filling the air with a sacred kind of peace.

"How about a little walk?" Ethan said slowly and brightly, crouching beside her. His voice carried that familiar warmth, always bright and playful, as though coaxing a smile out of her was his daily mission.

Clara's mother blinked at him, her expression briefly confused. "A walk? I don't know if I can…" She hesitated, her voice trailing off.

"It's just a short stroll," He assured her gently. "Or you can sit on the bench and boss me around while I pull weeds—which one will it be?" Clara's mother chuckled softly, her mood lightened by his teasing. "I don't need to boss you around!" Ethan never treated her mother as just a patient, but more like a friend—or an important member of the family.

Clara sat quietly nearby, her face turned toward them, listening to the easy rhythm of their exchange. Each day, she heard Ethan speak to her mother in this way—teasing, cajoling, infusing her confusion with little sparks of humor and joy. Though she couldn't see the scene, she could hear the way her mother's laughter bubbled up, breaking through the fog of dementia, and it touched her deeply every time.

Ethan guided her mother carefully toward the bench by the flower beds, speaking to her as though they were old friends. "See these marigolds?" he said as they walked slowly. "They're bright orange, just like the sun when it sets. I planted them for you, you know, so you could have a little piece of sunshine even on cloudy days."

The mother laughed again, shaking her head. "You're a sweet talker, aren't you? I bet you say that to all the ladies." Her mother laughed again, shaking her head. Ethan looked at her, his heart swelling with emotion as he realized her mind had momentarily returned to the present, grounding her in the real world. "Only the ones who make the best tea," Ethan quipped with a grin. "And since you're the reigning

*The Third Eye*

champion, I've got to stay on your good side."

Clara couldn't help but smile, her heart filled with warmth. She didn't need her eyes to see the love and care he poured into every word and action. She felt it in the way he spoke to her mother, in the way he made even the smallest moments feel meaningful. She felt it in the way he described the world to her now, painting pictures with his words that she could hold in her mind like treasures.

Suddenly her mother say to Ethan, "You are so nice, dear," in a soft voice, tinged with sincerity.

"Thank you, Mom," he said, his voice quieter now, almost tender. "But you and Clara make it easy. This house feels more like a home with you both here."

Clara felt a deep warmth spread through her chest when she heard Ethan address her mother as "Mom." The word slipped from his lips so naturally, so effortlessly, as though it had always belonged there. Yet, it wasn't just the familiarity of the word that struck her—it was the way he said it, with a tenderness and sincerity that made it feel whole, unforced, and filled with love.

The mother, whose mind often wandered into foggy places, didn't always catch the significance, but Clara did. She felt it deeply. The way he said "Mom" carried a weight of love that Clara hadn't expected but now couldn't imagine living without. He didn't just care for her mother out of kindness; he embraced her as family, as someone worth loving, even in the midst of her brokenness and confusion.

Clara smiled, her voice trembling slightly as she spoke. "Honey," she called softly, her tone filled with emotion.

"Yes?" he replied, turning to face her.

"Thank you for calling her Mom," she said, her words simple but heavy with meaning. "It means more than I can say." Ethan's voice was steady, but there was a gentleness to it that matched the moment perfectly. "She's our mom, honey. I say it because I mean it."

Clara felt her throat tighten again, tears threatening to spill. She didn't need her sight to know that he was smiling at her, the kind of smile that wasn't just on his lips but in his heart.

# A QUIET ACHE

In Ethan's gentle care and the way he embraced her mother as his own, Clara found not just comfort but a deep, abiding joy. Even in the midst of their struggles, moments like these reminded her that love—the kind of love Ethan gave so freely—had the power to heal in ways words could never fully capture.

*** 

Filipe, now a biologist working in a local laboratory, paid a visit to his old friend Ethan and Clara. He had changed over the years, his life having taken a more scientific path, but his friendship with Ethan had remained constant, unwavering through time. As he stepped through the door of Ethan's home, he was greeted by the familiar warmth of a place that always felt like a refuge. Clara was sitting quietly by the window, her presence peaceful, almost ethereal.

"Filipe!" Ethan greeted, his voice a mix of relief and joy. The two men embraced as old friends do, with a sense of knowing that only comes from years of shared experiences.

Filipe, despite his scientific career, had always been drawn to deeper conversations, those that went beyond the surface. He looked at Clara, who was silently observing the world outside, and remarked, "I've always wondered, Ethan, how you manage to find such stillness in a world that's constantly moving. You've learned something I can't quite grasp."

Ethan smiled, his gaze shifting to Clara. "It's not about controlling the world around you. It's about learning to sit with the silence. Clara has taught me that. Sometimes, the answers come when you stop looking so hard for them."

Clara, with her gentle wisdom, nodded slightly, as though confirming Ethan's words without speaking a sound. Filipe, who had spent years in a world driven by data and analysis, paused to consider this. "I spend my days in a laboratory, surrounded by facts and figures, trying to make sense of the natural world," he said. "But there's something about this peaceful stillness you've found that I can't explain with logic. It's like you've discovered something beyond what science can measure."

Ethan leaned back in his chair, his eyes thoughtful. "Science has its place, Filipe. But peace... that's something

*The Third Eye*

different. It's about understanding what you can't see, the things that can't be measured with a microscope or calculated with a formula."

Filipe, always the curious one, nodded. "I've spent years analyzing life at a cellular level, but I've often wondered about the intangible parts of existence—the things you can't see but that shape everything."

Clara's voice, soft as a whisper, cut through the conversation. "Some things... you can only feel. You can't analyze the wind or measure a sunset. But you can experience them, deeply. And in that experience, you find the answers."

Filipe smiled at her, appreciating her words. "You've both taught me something today. Maybe it's not all about finding answers or solving problems. Maybe it's about living in the questions, letting them guide you."

As the afternoon wore on, their conversation deepened. Filipe shared stories of his work in the lab, the discoveries and the challenges, but it was clear that the real conversation was happening in the spaces between words, in the moments of silence. The three of them, connected by years of friendship, understood that some of the most meaningful discussions happen not in solving problems, but in simply being together and listening.

The conversation flowed easily between Ethan, Filipe, and Clara, a blend of stories, laughter, and reflections. But just as they were beginning to dive into deeper topics, the sharp ring of the phone cut through the peaceful atmosphere. Ethan's face changed as he looked at the screen, then glanced apologetically at his friends.

"It's from the hospital," he said, his voice steady but urgent. "I've to go. Filipe, please stay here with us. I'll be back soon."

Without waiting for a response, Ethan hurriedly grabbed his coat and left, the door closing behind him with a soft click. The room was left in a quiet stillness. Clara and Filipe sat across from one another, the gentle hum of the house the only sound now.

Filipe sat back for a moment, his gaze thoughtful as he searched for the right words. His voice, usually steady and

# A QUIET ACHE

confident, was softer now, tinged with the weight of the memories he was about to share. "You know, Clara," he began, "I've known Ethan for years, deeply, and I can see just how much he's always loved you. It's something that's never really faded, no matter how much time has passed." He paused, collecting his thoughts before continuing. "I've always admired his patience and endurance, especially through those long years—both during high school and after. It wasn't easy for him. But even then, I could see the quiet strength in him, how he carried that love for you without expecting anything in return."

Filipe's voice softened even more as he spoke, as if he were revisiting those old, hidden moments. "Back in high school, when things were tough for him, he would talk about you often. He never mentioned it directly, of course—Ethan's never been one to express his feelings openly. But I could see it in the way his eyes would light up when he spoke about you, even if he was only sharing a passing memory. It was like a longing he didn't know how to express, a silent ache. And I knew, even then, how much he was holding on to you, how much he missed you."

Clara's breath caught slightly as Filipe's words sank in. For a moment, she was silent, her expression unreadable, as if processing something that had always been there but had never fully reached her until now. The stillness between them deepened, and she gently touched her hand to her chest, a soft gesture as though grounding herself in the revelation.

"I... I never knew," she finally whispered, her voice soft, almost fragile. "I never knew Ethan felt that way. Not like this." Her fingers curled slightly, as if to hold onto the reality of what Filipe had just shared.

Filipe, sensing her contemplation, smiled softly. "You know," he began, his voice gentle, "I've always believed that love finds us when we least expect it. But with you two, it feels different. It feels like it was always meant to be, even when it seemed impossible."

Clara nodded, her heart swelling with the weight of his words. "I never thought I'd be here," she whispered, her voice tinged with emotion. "There was a time when I didn't think I deserved this. I didn't think I could be the woman he needed after everything I put him through."

Filipe's hand rested gently on hers. "You've always been the woman he needed. He saw you in a way no one else did. And you've always seen him, too. Even when you couldn't see with your eyes now, you saw him with your heart. That's what brought you back closer together. Seeing others through the heart allows for deeper understanding and empathy."

Clara's head dropped, and a tear escaped down her cheek. She hadn't realized how much she had needed to hear those words, how much she had needed to understand that, despite all the pain and the years apart, the love they shared was still enough. It was more than enough. It was everything.

Her head tilted down slightly, a faint, bittersweet smile tugging at the corners of her lips. "All these years, I thought... I thought I was the one holding onto something, that I was the one missing something, but he..." Her voice trailed off, overwhelmed by the quiet emotion she had never allowed herself to fully understand.

Filipe, watching her closely, noticed how her face expression softened as she processed the weight of his words. "He's always loved you, Clara," Filipe continued gently, as if giving her space to absorb the depth of the truth. "I have been with him since childhood, so I understand him the most. He never said it outright, but he carried it with him. Quietly, always."

She was silent for a moment longer, the weight of this revelation settling into her heart, mingling with the memories she had kept locked away. Her voice, when she spoke again, was quieter, tinged with a quiet vulnerability. "I didn't know, but now I do..."

Clara lowered her head, her heart heavy with deep sorrow about many things.

Filipe watched Clara, his heart heavy with empathy for her. He could see the mix of awe and sorrow in her expression, the realization that something she had never fully understood was now coming to light. Filipe, sensing the weight of Clara's sorrow, gently spoke, his voice filled with empathy. "I can only imagine how hard it must have been for you, Clara," he said softly. "Ethan's silence, all those years... I know it wasn't easy. Sometimes, silence speaks louder than words, especially when it's filled with unspoken love, longing, and patience. Ethan never meant to hurt you. He just... waited... waited. He carried his feelings for you quietly, hoping the right time would come."

Filipe continued, his voice gentle yet filled with deep understanding, " you were not just a memory for him; you were his quiet, hidden motivation. In the silence, when he missed you the most, and at times when hopelessness crept in, he realized something important—that he needed to heal others who were broken, wounded, and longing, just as he had felt. That realization became his driving force, his greatest motivation to push through the challenges he could hardly have imagined. If I were him, I would have collapsed. I know him well, Clara. It was his love, your absence, and the yearning for you that gave him the strength to keep going, to face every hurdle with determination," Filipe spoke softly. "But I know it must have been a silent burden for you as well, wondering if you were even seen or understood."

Filipe understood that Clara was now confused about many things, particularly her need for space to reflect on Ethan's love and her sight loss. So, Filipe began to share his insights, offering her guidance as an old friend and a biology researcher, his gaze softening as he recognized the sadness in her. "You know, I've spent my life studying living beings, trying to understand the mysteries that make them whole. But even with all the research, there are things I can never fully grasp. I believe life is both a mystery and a grace. And, you two together is also a mystery."

Clara turned her head toward his voice, a small smile tugging at her lips. "I think I know what you mean, Filipe," she said softly. "I've come to understand that I can still 'see'—just in a different way now. The world speaks to me through sound, touch, and scent. I feel it in the rustling of leaves, the fresh scent after rain, the warmth of the sun on my skin. I don't need my eyes to experience all of that."

Filipe nodded, his eyes filled with understanding. "It's a beautiful way to see the world. I've spent years studying the

## The Third Eye

earth, but I've never really *felt* it like you do. The way you experience the rhythm of the earth beneath you, the vibrations in the air, the whispers of nature that most people miss... it's a vision that others can't always understand." Filipe believed that blindness could be compensated for by enhanced hearing or other heightened abilities.

Clara paused, her fingers twitching slightly as if trying to find the right words to say. "It's true," she said, her voice steady. "I've learned to see with my heart, with my senses. And sometimes, it feels like the world is more alive now than it ever was before. It's as if my eyes weren't the only way to truly see."

Filipe smiled softly, a quiet admiration in his eyes. "You've found a way to see that most people don't. You've tuned into a deeper, more profound frequency. And that's something no one can take from you."

***

A month had passed since Filipe's visit to Ethan and Clara, and everything seemed to be falling into place.

It was a glorious day, the sun bathing the earth in a beautiful light, as if the world were pausing in anticipation of what was about to happen.

Clara sat on the edge of the small lake, feeling the warmth of the day and listening to the gentle whispers of the wind. Ethan was beside her, his presence a steady comfort, but there was something in the air today—a quiet anticipation, a shift she couldn't quite explain.

Sitting there, Ethan's arm wrapped around Clara's waist, while his other hand held hers gently, both of them breathing in the natural scent of the lake and surrounding trees, their hearts finding a quiet rhythm in the stillness of the moment.

Ethan, after a brief pause, stood up slowly, his voice soft but certain when he spoke. "Honey, there's something I've wanted to ask you for a long time, something that I've carried with me." He reached into his pocket, pulling out a small velvet box. Clara's heart raced, her breath catching in her chest. She could feel the moment shifting, the world narrowing down to this single, profound instant.

Ethan knelt before her, his voice thick with emotion.

## A QUIET ACHE

"Clara, I love you. I've loved you for as long as I can remember, through everything. I've waited for the right moment to ask you—Will you marry me? Will you share your life with me, for all that it is, and all that it will be?"

Clara's heart shattered and soared all at once. Her mind raced, and for a moment, all the memories of the pain she had caused, the scars she had left, flooded her thoughts. *How could he still love me?* she thought. *I left him so many wounds, so many unanswered years. I don't deserve this love, this future.*

Her lips trembled, but the words she wanted to say wouldn't come. She didn't feel worthy of the love he was offering, but her heart, her soul, screamed with the desperate truth that she had never stopped loving him, even when she had walked away. The silence between them was heavy, filled with everything she couldn't voice.

With a trembling hand, she gently touched his, her response not in words, but in the quiet, tear-filled nod she gave him. The tears slipped down her face, each one a silent testament to the love she had never truly allowed herself to believe in. She didn't speak. She couldn't. But in that moment, her entire being was saying "yes"—yes to the man who had stood by her through everything, yes to a future she never believed she was worthy of. Yet, deep down, she felt he deserved someone far better and more beautiful than herself.

Without a word, she threw herself into his arms, holding him tightly as the tears flowed freely. The weight of years, of missed chances, of unspoken love, all seemed to dissolve in the embrace. Ethan held her just as tightly, his heart full of a love that had waited so long, patiently and quietly, to be returned.

Now, as he looked at her, he felt a quiet certainty settle within him. The love he had once thought hopeless was now his greatest source of strength. He didn't need to seek fulfillment in other places or people, because he had found it in the simple, yet profound act of giving himself to her, to their shared life. And in that, he realized, he had found the meaning of happiness—a happiness that had always been there, waiting to be discovered, through love, and through giving.

He knew, with unwavering certainty, that she was everything to him—his entire world, his everything.

And now, he deeply understood his father's words: *Trust that everything will fall into place.* For so long, Ethan had struggled with doubt, trying to control every aspect of his life. But in this moment, standing beside her, he saw the truth in his father's wisdom. Life had unfolded in ways he never could have planned or imagined, and yet, here he was, exactly where he needed to be. Trusting in the journey, in the love they shared, had brought him peace—a peace that could only come from surrendering to life's flow, knowing that, in time, everything would fall into place.

*\*\*\**

It was late afternoon, the same day of their life commitment—a day of quiet purpose, Ethan and Filipe, united by deep friendship, worked side by side to prepare an intimate gathering at Ethan's parents' home. Each element, from the delicate arrangement of flowers by Ethan's mother to the thoughtful placement of chairs, was imbued with sincerity, reflecting the love at the heart of the day.

The air was filled with calm anticipation as they carefully arranged every detail. The home, filled with the peaceful light of the setting sun, radiated warmth and simplicity.

What made the evening even more special was Ethan's contribution—a collection of songs Clara had sung long ago. With care, he compiled them into a playlist, ready to play through the CD player that evening. The music, with its heartfelt tones, would fill the gathering with a sense of family intimacy and shared joy. Ethan, aware of music's profound ability to heal and connect, knew it was a perfect touch. It was a universal language, one that transcended differences and spoke directly to the soul, reminding Clara and every one of life's hope and the strength of love.

Ethan's parents, watching their son's quiet determination and resilience, couldn't help but feel both pride and admiration.

Later, as the evening mellowed, Filipe stepped outside with Ethan, the cool breeze brushing past them. The stars above seemed to reflect the questions stirring in Filipe's

## A QUIET ACHE

mind. For too long, he had wrestled with a thought he hadn't dared to voice. But now, standing side by side in the comfort of their deep friendship, he felt ready to speak. "I've always known that most men love women when they're young and beautiful," Filipe began, his voice laced with hesitation. "But ... she's lost her sight, broken in so many ways. I just don't understand why you've held onto your love for her all these years."

Ethan turned to Filipe, his gaze steady, his expression calm yet thoughtful. He paused briefly before speaking, as though summoning a memory deeply etched in his heart. "My father once shared a story with me—something I've carried with me all my life," he said, his voice soft yet firm. "He asked me, 'Is an old, wrinkled $100 bill the same as a brand-new one?' Of course, the answer is yes. They might look different on the outside, but their value remains unchanged."

Ethan let the weight of his words settle before continuing, his tone filled with quiet conviction. "It's the same with people, Filipe. We might lose our youth, our beauty, even parts of ourselves, but our value—our essence—never changes. That's why I still love her. Not for how she looks, not for what she can or can't do, but for who she is. And that's why I always will."

Filipe nodded slowly, the words sinking in, filling the quiet night with their truth. He could see Ethan's unwavering love in a new light—a love not bound by time or circumstance but rooted in something far deeper.

Later that evening, surrounded by their closest ones—Clara's mother, Ethan's parents, and Filipe—the room was filled with laughter, joy, and the quiet hum of a love renewed. Clara's heart, the happiest it had been in a long time, swelled as she felt the warmth of their support, their presence a reminder that even when one part of her world had been taken away, there were still so many ways to feel loved, connected, and seen.

Before joining in the humble yet meaningful celebration of their engagement, Ethan turned to his parents and said softly, "Dad, Mom, let's say grace first." Ethan's mother smiled warmly, touched by how her son always recognized

# The Third Eye

the presence of Someone behind it all.

The room fell into a sacred silence, and then the father slowly began to say grace, thanking God for the gift of life, for the happiness of his two children in His blessing, and for everyone gathered, all under God's loving care and plan.

As the prayer ended, Clara's mother suddenly turned to embrace her daughter, then Ethan. She seemed more alert, as if something deep within her had been awakened.

Filipe, radiating joy without a hint of restraint, raised his glass in a heartfelt toast. His voice was steady and full of affection. "To love," he said, "and to the strength of the human heart that finds its way, no matter the distance or the years." Then, everyone laughed joyfully, the sound filling the room.

Clara deeply felt the weight of the moment—of the love that surrounded her, of the life she was about to build with Ethan. And for the first time, she allowed herself to believe that she deserved this love, that the future they would share would be beautiful, despite all the struggles they had faced.

As the evening continued, Clara found herself surrounded by a warmth that had nothing to do with the physical world. The laughter of the loved ones, the soft voices of Ethan's parents sharing stories of their younger days, Clara's mother offering her cute smiles, Filipe joyfully playing the role of the merry maker—all of it melded into a comforting symphony of belonging. Though she could not see, Clara felt it all deeply, as though every word, every touch, was an affirmation of the life that was slowly unfolding before her.

Ethan, giving Clara and Filipe a moment alone, quietly stepped away to speak with Clara's mother. "I have two moms now, thank you for everything, and thank you for giving me Clara," he expressed sincerely, then gave her forehead a kiss. She gave a warm, big smile, holding his hand tightly, then he joined his parents.

Filipe and Clara, bound by a sacred friendship, shared a brief but meaningful conversation. Clara's fingers traced the edge of the ring on her finger, the cool metal a constant reminder of the promise Ethan had made. It wasn't just a symbol of their engagement; it was a symbol of everything

## A QUIET ACHE

they had overcome, every moment of doubt that had been shattered by the strength of their love.

As the evening wore on, the conversation flowed around them like a gentle stream. The laughter grew louder, the jokes more frequent, but Clara remained still, her heart full of the quiet certainty that had settled within her. She knew now that love wasn't about perfection. It wasn't about never making mistakes. It was about finding someone who would walk beside you, even when the road was difficult, even when the world seemed too dark to navigate.

A few tears slipped down her cheek.

During this beautiful evening, her natural voice, playing softly from the CD player, filled the room, warming her heart with gratitude for the gifts God had bestowed upon her—both the ability to share her voice with others and the gift of hearing. She felt Ethan's presence beside her, and without a word, he took her hand in his, his touch warm and reassuring. It was the touch of a man who had loved her through the years, through the silence, the pain, and… through everything.

And as they stood there, surrounded by the people who cared for them, Clara felt a sense of peace. She realized that love could only be seen through the third eye, not the physical ones. It was a love that transcended vision, felt deeply in the heart and soul, and could see beyond the surface. She understood, with quiet clarity, that love truly bears all things—enduring the pain, the brokenness, and even the deepest scars, transforming them into something stronger and more profound.

Ethan reflected on all he had witnessed throughout his years as a doctor, a profound understanding washed over him. He had cared for so many people—each one with a unique story, each one carrying burdens he couldn't fully comprehend. He had seen the rich and the poor, the educated and the uneducated, the successful and those who had lost everything. Despite the vast differences in their lives, they all shared one unspoken truth: the most important things in life weren't things at all.

He had watched them endure unimaginable pain, often

losing everything they thought mattered—health, wealth, status, loved ones—and yet, in their darkest moments, they found something deeper. Some found peace in forgiveness, others in acceptance, but all of them found strength in love. The love they gave, the love they received, the love they carried even when everything else seemed lost.

He realized, with quiet clarity, that this was the lesson life had been teaching him all along. The value of love and human connection wasn't measured by success, or possessions, or status—but by the strength to keep going in the face of loss, and the courage to open your heart, even when it felt impossible.

He thought of Clara, and how her journey mirrored those of his patients. She, too, was losing something—something deeply important to her. But just as those he had cared for had found resilience and hope in the face of the impossible, so too would Clara find her way. The price of this lesson was steep, and life had demanded much of them both, but in the end, it was clear. The greatest lessons in life came not from what we kept, but from what we were willing to give up, to let go, and to love despite it all.

As he thought of the road ahead, he knew that this lesson—the one that had been quietly whispered to him through the lives of those he had cared for—was the greatest blessing of all. Life was not about what was lost, but what was found in the spaces between, in the love that endures, and in the quiet moments of strength when all seems lost. And with that understanding, Ethan's heart swelled with a deep, quiet peace, knowing that together, Clara and he could face whatever came next.

As they stood on the precipice of this new chapter, Ethan thought of the families he had witnessed over the years—those like Filipe's mother and his own parents, whose love had endured the trials of life and had only grown stronger in the process. The greatest gift they had given him was not just their love, but the way they had shaped the meaning of family, of togetherness, and of the legacy of love that was passed down to the next generation. Ethan could see it now, how much more precious that gift had become as he thought

## A QUIET ACHE

of the future with Clara—one where they might have children of their own.

The idea of raising a child together seemed more than just an aspiration; it was a bridge, a way to deepen their bond, to solidify the love they had nurtured in the quiet moments and the storms. A child would be the embodiment of their love, a treasure greater than diamonds, something forged not through wealth or success, but through the sacrifices, the growth, and the resilience they had shared. The laughter of a child, the warmth of small hands in theirs, would be a reminder of all they had endured and overcome.

As Ethan looked at Clara, he saw not just the woman he loved, but the great mother she would one day be—someone who would pass down the strength, the tenderness, and the quiet wisdom that had brought them this far. And together, they would create a future where love was their legacy, a future where their children would grow up knowing that love—real love—was about more than just what you received, but what you gave, what you built, and what you passed on.

The future, once uncertain and clouded with doubt, now stretched out before Ethan and Clara—clear, bright, and full of possibility. It was a future they would build together, one step at a time.

With Ethan beside her, she knew that every challenge they faced from here on out would be met not in solitude, but together, their hearts intertwined in a bond stronger than anything they had ever known. And in that quiet, shared moment, they realized that love—true, unwavering love—was not just about surviving the storms, but about learning how to dance in the rain, side by side.

Now, in this moment, Ethan knew he was the happiest of them all, always staying close to Clara, her hand resting in his. His mind wandered to the profound joy of being with her after all those long years of quiet ache.

And in that same moment, Clara, with the eye of her soul and all the love in her heart, was ready to take that first step.

Manufactured by Amazon.ca
Acheson, AB